The Protectors

by

April Hollingworth

The Candi Reynolds Series

The Protectors

Cover Art by *Debbie Taylor*

The Wild Rose Press, Inc.
PO Box 708
Adams Basin, NY 14410-0708
Visit us at www.thewildrosepress.com

Publishing History
First Mainstream Paranormal Edition, 2017
Print ISBN 978-1-5092-1472-3
Digital ISBN 978-1-5092-1473-0

The Candi Reynolds Series, Book 3
Published in the United States of America

"I'll never let you go,"

he informs me as he drags me back toward him. "You are mine and I am yours. End of discussion."

"There was a discussion in there somewhere?"

Flipping me over as easily as if I'm a pancake in a pan, he gives me one more yank so my butt is at the edge of the bed, and his large body is wedged between my legs. Leaning forward, he grasps hold of my chin, keeping my face still, and maintains eye contact with me.

"No discussion, just a simple fact. You keep trying to run from your feelings, and I'm not letting you anymore," he growls the words out, practically spitting them in my face. "So you need me, and you're afraid of the fact. Fair enough. Now let me tell you something, little girl. I need you too."

"Little girl?" I manage to sputter out before being harshly interrupted.

"Yes. You are mine. Your body, mind, and your fucking soul, is mine. Get used to it, sweetheart, because I'm never letting you go." Next thing I know, his mouth has slammed down on mine. His kiss is one of punishment and domination. There's no gentleness in it at all.

Strangely enough, it's exactly what I need. I need to feel and hear that he's on this emotional roller-coaster with me. I know he loves me. He's far from afraid of telling me, *unlike me*, but seeing this fury and dominance coming from him is spelling out loud and clear what he's feeling, and it's like I suddenly know everything is going to be okay.

Dedication

I'd like to dedicate this book to you, the reader.
Thank you for coming on this adventure with me.

Chapter 1

I can't believe we're going to New Orleans to find others to help us in the coming war against The Protectors. Looking around the room at my friends and fellow warriors, I still feel shocked over the latest events. We've been through so much together in such a short amount of time.

My best friend Jasmine, an Alsatian shifter, had been trapped in her animal form until a few short months ago, when we met werewolf Detective Kheda McKnight and Victor Harlow, vampire most scrumptious, especially with his unique silvery-green eyes that turn vampiric blue when his emotions change, and the first man whom I've let into my life and heart.

The four of us worked together in solving some brutal murders, and in the process, Jasmine and Kheda almost died.

Then we dragged in the extra help of Jasmine's and my fellow Sisters in Arms. Necromancer Selene Holden and her twin sister, Nancy, who was a necromancer until she was brought back to life as a zombie.

Add in Felicity McCormack and Talia Thompson, otherwise known as T.T., who are both talented witches. Werewolf shifter Vivian Dwight and jaguar shifter Jezebel O'Malley, who's currently in New Orleans with the sexy and persistent bounty hunter Cedrix O'Laughlan.

Cedrix had followed Jezebel to Ireland so he could drag her back before a warrant went out for her skipping bail. Except things didn't go quite how he expected, what with him finding out magick and shifters and all things that go bump in the night actually exist, and that he's a witch too.

My gaze drifts to the final three people in the room, which brings my thoughts to the strangest thing to happen over the last few months. The visions I was having. Visions that literally took me into the past to see events unfold and gather clues to answers to questions leading to the truth about Vincent, Victor's vampire brother and best friend. Answers about the Warrioress Daphmire Janna and the fact that I'm descended from both her children, the only one in all the centuries to carry the special double magick. How weird is that?

And if that wasn't strange enough, we rescued Janna's and Vincent's ten-year-old daughter Roísín; who was kidnapped by Vincent's mother and sold to humans working for *The Protectors*. To say these past few weeks have flown by is laughable. It has been bizarre, gritty, and at times darn embarrassing. Yet it has also been exhilarating, intriguing, and one hell of an eye opener.

Which brings us to the here and now, an abandoned house we commandeered for our safe house.

The house was spelled to hide our presence and the room that holds the book of prophecies we searched so hard for. Anyone looking at it would see nothing more than an old and empty house.

Looking around, I can't help feeling a sense of excitement wash through me.

"Come on, Candi, we best gather our stuff together and head for the airport." Victor traces his fingers along my face, down my neck, over my shoulder, and down my arm until he can link his fingers with me. He gives my fingers a gentle squeeze before pulling me away from the book of Prophecies.

As everyone turns to exit the room, I suddenly pause and look over my shoulder, but not at the book. We've already copied everything we need from it. Instead, my gaze rests on the wall which holds a huge family tree. My family tree, to be exact; for some reason, I can't leave it behind.

I loosen my fingers from Victor's, walk back, reach up, and unpin the family tree. I'm surprised to realize it's made from the softest leather. A moment later, Victor helps me carefully roll it up. Once done, we follow the others through the hidden door, which looks like part of the wall when viewed from the other side, and head back downstairs.

With a final look around, I whisper, "Hide once more." I watch as all furniture flickers out of view leaving the house looking empty, yet the feeling of it being full remains.

****

"We need to spell the weapons," mutters Felicity, to me as we hurry into the airport.

"Shit, okay, hold up a sec, guys," I call out to the others, making our large group pause. They hurry back to where Felicity and I wait. Before any of them can ask questions, we quickly start spelling the weapons so they will be invisible to all types of detection, both human and electronic. The third witch in our group, T.T, quickly joins in, making the process more efficient and quicker.

"Okay, let's go," she informs everyone once the spells are in place.

We hurry to security, walk through without any hassles, and then hurry to catch our plane. Well, to be more exact, Janna's plane, as she not only owns it, she's also the pilot. Seriously cool.

Once we're all on board and our luggage is stowed away, I grab a seat and Victor sits beside me. Roísín sits across from me and graces me with a shy smile. Ever since her rescue yesterday, she's been staying close to me. I find it confusing as I've had no previous dealings with children. To be honest, I have no idea what to say to her.

"So, umm, you okay?" I tentatively ask. After all, she has just gone through six months of God only knows what at the hands of the humans holding her. I'm just grateful she wasn't with the other supernaturals being held captive and tortured.

"I'm good, thanks to you."

"Ugh umm." I tilt my head sideways and look at her, unsure what to say. I let my gaze slide sideways toward the vampire beside me who watches this interaction with a smile.

"You saved me, came for me, and took me away from them. If it wasn't for you…"

Leaning forward, I make sure she's looking me directly in the eye. "Look, kid, your parents are the ones who saved you, never stopped searching for you. They love you so much. I hope you know that." It's only because I'm staring her in the eyes I see the flash of longing and hope flicker, before being squished. Her bottom lip trembles slightly before she determinedly stops even that slight telltale of emotion.

"How can I know for sure they love me?" she whispers so quietly I almost don't hear her words. I'm thankful I did hear them.

"Because they do love you, more than anything in the world. Your being kidnapped almost tore them apart. They had one clue, and they never stopped chasing after it. Never stopped looking for you. They love you so much," I inform the now silently crying girl.

I feel my hand being picked up, fingers entwined, and a reassuring pressure of a squeeze. I'll take that as meaning I did well with my reassuring.

Chapter 2

The flight is thankfully uneventful. I watch as Roísín sits quietly in her seat except to now and again turn her head toward the cockpit where both her parents sit.

Finally, after four and a half hours of flying, she asks the question she obviously wants to know.

"I know my mum is the pilot and has to fly the plane, but why does my dad have to be in there too. Why can't he be out here with me?"

"Oh, sweetie, your father is the copilot. Both your parents are needed in the cockpit to fly the plane."

"Oh, so he's not hiding?"

"No, he most certainly isn't."

"It's just that they kept telling me they love me so much and how sorry they were for me being taken. They said how much they've missed me, and yet…"

"Would you like to see them?"

"Do you think that would be okay?" Uncertainty laces her voice, even as a hesitant smile pulls at the corner of her mouth.

"I don't think they'd mind at all," I reply. Unbuckling my belt, I hold my hand out for Roísín's. A moment later, her smaller hand curls into mine, and I marvel at the difference in our sizes.

Together, we cross to the cockpit and ease open the door. We stay for just a couple of minutes, yet enough time for Roísín to be comforted by her parents, and reassured once more of how much they love her. Upon returning to our seats, I watch as tension eases out of her little body, and a slight smile filled with hope flickers and then stays on her face. *Poor kid. Though thankfully, I do believe she is beginning to realize her parents do love her. Hopefully, she will be okay.*

"How do you know them, my parents?"

"Well, as it happens, Victor and your father grew up together. They have been estranged for a long, long time."

"Oh. And they just asked for your help?"

"Well, the thing is, we were there when they found out what your grandmother had done. We offered to help. Your parents were happy to accept our help."

"Oh, and then you found out we were related to each other. Are you my aunty?"

"Eh, no, to be honest, I think you are mine in a very, very distant way." I chuckle thinking just how many generations between her siblings and me there are.

"Does that mean I can tell you what to do?"

"No, it certainly does not."

I watch as she twists her mouth from side to side as she considers what she has learned.

"Okay. If I need you…will you help me?"

"If I can, I will. You do know, though, your parents will protect you."

Uncertainty flashes across her face, once more her eyes flicker toward the cockpit door before coming back to meet mine.

"How can I be certain? They let my grandmother take me away from them already. They might let her again."

"Oh, sweetie, they didn't let her take you away, and won't let anyone else either. They truly do love you very much."

For some reason, I'm not sure why, my words seem to sooth her. For the rest of the flight, she eases back into her chair and rests, until finally she drifts off to sleep.

An hour later, we've finally arrived in New Orleans, and Roísín is carried from the plane, still sleeping, cradled in her father's arms.

Chapter 3

Getting off the plane, I'm rather delighted to find it is quite warm. Entering the terminal building, we quickly go through customs. Sadly, Roísín must be woken up, bless her. She looks exhausted and can hardly keep her eyes open. We're met on the other side by Jezebel and Cedrix.

As a group, we hurry out of the airport and climb into a minivan Cedrix hired. Once Roísín's safely belted in between her parents, she cuddles up to Vincent, and I notice her hand linking with Janna's. Secure in her parents' embrace, she promptly falls asleep. Vincent pulls her closer to him and presses a gentle kiss on the top of her head. When he looks up, his gaze zeros straight toward Janna's. "She's finally safe," he whispers, as if he is only now allowing himself to believe it.

I turn away, leaving them to enjoy their moment of contentment. Climbing into my seat, I buckle up before asking the question I've been dying to ask.

"Jezebel, how did it go? I'm assuming you signed in on time as you're here."

"You were right. If I'd gone to Montana with you, I would have gotten myself thrown in jail for skipping bail," she grumbles.

"I wouldn't have let that happen," Cedrix growls from the driver's seat, causing everyone to pause in what they're doing and to turn and stare at him.

"You wouldn't?"

"No, I told you, I'll look out for you."

Hmmm, sounds like something interesting happened between them. I wonder what? We were only separated for three days. What the hell could have happened to make such a huge difference?

"I know, I just...thank you, I appreciate it," Jezebel replies, making me come out of my thoughts and zero back in on the conversation.

"So, what exactly did you two get up to while we were gone?" I casually ask.

I get an amused look from Victor, so I assume I wasn't as smooth and casual as I thought, especially with the snorts of laughter coming from behind me.

Turning around in my seat, I stare at the others before flashing them a cheeky grin. "Are any of you honestly going to say you aren't curious?"

"Hell, no, I'm dying to know what happened too," chuckles Vivian from her seat. "I just would have tried to ask in a less obvious way."

"I thought I did," I mutter in reply, only to have everyone burst out laughing.

"A sledgehammer would have been less obvious," Cedrix informs me with a deep chuckle.

I half think I should be offended, on principle, except he's probably right.

"Sooo, what did you get up to then?" I ask again, on receiving no answer except a wry look for my trouble. I let out a huff. "Ugh, fine, be that way, don't tell, see if I care. Where are we going?" I peer out the window at the beautiful old houses coming into view. I want to get out and explore everywhere.

"We're going to my house. It's near Lafayette Cemetery No. 1," Jezebel answers. A smile spreads across her face as she takes in our reactions.

"You live near the cemetery?" I finally ask in surprise. "You've always hated graveyards because they creeped you out!"

Bursting out laughing, she nods her head in agreement. "I know, right? Yet it's different here for some strange reason, not sure why. Anyway, I love my house. It's small, so it'll be a tight fit. You're all welcome to squeeze in for the duration."

"I have some room too. Between Jezebel's and my place, everyone will be at least able to sleep," Cedrix informs us, in his rather gruff matter-of-fact manner.

I can't help staring at him in surprise at such a generous offer.

"Thank you." I can hear the genuine gratitude in Victor's simple reply. Going by the nod of his head in acknowledgement, so can Cedrix.

We turn left on Washington Avenue across from Lafayette Cemetery and turn into Coliseum Street, where a couple of houses down we pull in front of a beautiful two-story house with a cherry blossom tree out front. I gape in delight at the old iron balcony. Painted in white with pale pink around the door and window frames, the house is beautiful and delicate looking.

"Wow, Jezebel, this is gorgeous," T.T exclaims, surprise echoing in her voice and written on her face.

"What were you expecting? A rundown house? A shack fallen down around my ears?"

"No, no, don't get me wrong, it's just this place is…"

"Feminine, delicate, and something you normally don't allow to be shown where you're concerned," interrupts Vivian.

"Huh, yeah, okay, I get where you're coming from. Thing is, ever since moving to New Orleans, I've felt as if I've finally found 'me.' I'm able to be who I really am supposed to be," Jezebel admits quietly.

"I'm glad you finally found somewhere that sets you free." Turning to my friend, I lean over the seat and place a hand on her shoulder. "And I have to admit, this place is gorgeous. I can understand why it calls to you so strongly."

On this note, we all exit the minivan. Turning once more to Jezebel, I ask the question foremost on my mind. "How many of us can stay here?"

"Well, some of you will have to bunk together. I have room for eight of you to stay comfortably. Well, nine if Roísín stays in your room with you." The last is said to Janna and Vincent, who readily agree.

"I was thinking if Jasmine, Kheda, and Vivian all stay with Cedrix, you'll have somewhere to run when you shift into your other forms during tonight's full moon. Maybe you should also go with them too, Candi. I wasn't sure if you wanted to be near the cemetery though. I know how much you like them."

"I'd rather stay here. I really want to go exploring," I admit.

"You'll have to go on a tour as it's not open to the public otherwise, unless you sneak in at night." The last part of this statement is muttered so no one can overhear it.

In the end, Nancy, Selene, Felicity, T.T., Vincent, Janna, and Roísín, and Victor and I remove our bags from the minivan, while the others leave theirs inside it, before entering Jezebel's home.

I can't help admiring the place. Decorated minimally, the original architecture is displayed to the best advantage. We're shown our rooms and deposit our bags before heading back downstairs, toward the kitchen where everyone is grabbing something to drink.

"How about we all go to my place, get rid of your bags—" Cedrix nods to the three who are staying at his place, before carrying on. "—and grab something to eat in the French Quarter?"

"Sounds good to me," Kheda readily agrees. The rest of us quickly chorus our agreement too. "So where do you live?"

"The bayou," Cedrix replies, leaving me feeling slightly confused. After all, isn't the bayou a really big place with gators and stuff?

Once more, we pile into the minivan. This time headed to a place that to me sounds both wild and kinda cool. *Maybe I should have stayed there after all. Mind you, I can't wait to do some late night exploring of Lafayette Cemetery.*

Chapter 4

It takes forty-five minutes to get from Jezebel's place to where Cedrix lives on Victory Road at the very edge of the bayou. Looking out the window, all I see is the wild beauty of untamed natural swamp land. His nearest neighbors are farther down the road, close enough if he needs them, yet far enough away to keep his privacy.

His house is made from wood and stone. A double garage/boathouse takes up the ground floor. Stairs at the back lead upstairs to his front door. Once inside, I'm initially surprised how bright it is until I spy the large windows taking up most of the walls. Cedrix's place is minimalist, comfortable, and masculine with some beautiful paintings of the bayou on the walls.

Spotting a painting of an alligator coming out of the water with the trees behind bending as if a breeze is rustling through them, I'm truly impressed at how realistic it is. You can almost smell the water and feel the wind brushing by.

"Wow, this is awesome," I blurt out from where I'm standing directly in front of the painting.

"Thank you. I must admit I'm pleased with how it came out."

"Say what?" exclaims Jezebel, while I just turn around to gape at him. "You're the artist? Blimey, I've seen some of your paintings around town in a couple of cafés and have always admired them. I would never have guessed…"

"That I was an artist? Most people don't know; so why would you?"

"I don't know. I just feel like I should have known." Shaking her head, she turns away to stare at the painting I was admiring a minute ago.

I get the distinct feeling that her not guessing his artistic nature is troubling her, though for the life of me I can't figure out why.

"So how about I show you your rooms, and then we can go grab something to eat in town. Personally, I'm after a fully dressed po'boy."

"A what? Are you taking the mickey, or is there really something called a po'boy?" I demand in genuine curiosity. I do love trying new foods.

Cedrix shakes his head in amusement. A smile curls his full lips as a chuckle rumbles from him, catching all females' attention in the room. *What is it about men chuckling that draws our attention so fast?*

"A po'boy is a traditional New Orleans sandwich, normally made with fried shrimp or roast beef. Fully dressed is with everything in it, though you can have it half dressed too."

"Mmm, yum, what's fully dressed contain, though?" I can feel my eyes getting bigger just at the thought of fried shrimp, and my taste buds getting ready to water and explode in anticipation.

"Fully dressed is lettuce, tomatoes, pickles, onions, and any dressing you want to go with it. I recommend aioli."

"Okay, I'm sold; I'm having a po'boy, minus the pickles though." Scrunching up my nose and shaking my head I admit, "I don't like pickles." I get a horrified look from Cedrix as if I've somehow offended the delicious sounding po'boy. Honestly, I don't think the sandwich will mind.

Chapter 5

An hour later, my nose is twitching and my mouth watering, as different scents assail my senses with unbelievably delicious aromas. I notice the others in my group seem to be anticipating our coming meal as much as I am, going by their grumbling stomachs and wide-eyed looks of appreciation and longing as different platters are delivered to the surrounding tables.

Finally, our meals arrive, not that we've been waiting for ages, because we haven't. It's just the anticipation of trying the food getting to me. I'm beginning to have visions of leaping at a server and devouring everything they're bringing to someone else.

I slather my po'boy in hot sauce before picking it up and taking the first bite. Flavors erupt in my mouth bringing a groan of satisfaction from me. I could really get used to Southern cuisine. Twenty minutes later, I'm rubbing my stomach in satisfaction and to help ease my meal down on its merry path.

"So, what did you think?" Cedrix asks me while wiping his mouth with a napkin.

"Delicious. I'm glad I had it. Now about beignets...?" A spluttering cough interrupts me. Turning to give Kheda a puzzled look and to make sure he's okay, I find Jasmine rubbing his back as she pops the last bite of her sandwich in her mouth.

Turning back to Cedrix, I continue, "Can we try

them and gumbo at some stage—oh, and a voodoo cocktail too?"

"Oh, thank God, I thought you wanted to eat them now!" wheezes Kheda, while a grinning Cedrix agrees to make sure we'll try everything on my list at some point.

I do notice that he too looks slightly relieved at finding out I didn't mean right now.

"How about going on a tour or something?" Victor inquires while smiling indulgently at me and stroking my leg in ever-increasing circles, starting from my knee and rising up my leg.

I feel my stomach tighten and my eyelids flutter half closed. At this point, I slap my hand over his large one, clamping it to my thigh before it travels farther north. Out of the corner of my eye, I see his unrepentant expression and a look of promise in his eyes.

Damn, it should be illegal for someone to be so darn sexy! Next thing I know, everyone is pushing their chairs back and standing. Feeling a little bewildered, it takes me a second to remember we decided to go on a tour. I look up into the amused eyes of my friends, and a slight blush heats my cheeks. Quickly standing, I stick my hand into my pocket to retrieve my money to pay for my lunch.

Once we're all paid up, we head outside and grab the tickets from the tour agent. While we're waiting for the tour to start, we wander around, checking out the voodoo shops and the stalls open nearby. I must admit, New Orleans is enchanting, vibrant, and intriguing.

As we're passing a fortune teller, she pauses in her reading to call out for us to come to her soon. Glancing at her, I see the aura of power vibrate around her. I'm not sure why I'm surprised she's the real deal. Maybe because most fortune tellers are fakes, maybe because she's tolling her business on the street.

Whatever the reason, it doesn't matter; this woman has power rippling off her in waves. Looking at her, I give a nod of my head to let her know I will be back. After all, any help she can give, even if it's a warning, will be helpful. Hopefully.

Chapter 6

Forty-five minutes later, we're standing in front of the tomb of Marie Laveau, the Voodoo Queen, and our guide is doing a ritual and blessing over everyone in the group. I'm just hoping it'll work.

As we wander through the cemetery, I can't help sensing the restless spirits. A couple of times, out of the corner of my eye, I see a presence flitting by. The feeling of power and unease is like a thick blanket covering the area around us. I'm not sure what is causing it and can't wait to explore later, minus the tour guide and bystanders.

****

The fear that had driven me to the airport, to escape Whitechapel, finally eases enough for me to figure out where to go. I need to speak to someone I can trust. Someone who will understand what plagues me. I've never felt doubt like this since my introduction to my duties as member of The Protectors. *It was my father who had been sent to show me how to do the ritual.*

Thinking back to that time, I realize it's understandable the same doubt presses on me once again. After all, it was her parents my father and I had been sent to eradicate. Now I find myself once more in a situation she is involved in. The only difference is The Protectors *don't know yet what she is. I find myself*

20

hoping somehow I can prevent her death, yet for me to do so...I need to speak to my sister. Decision made, I book the next flight to Paris.

****

I have this strange feeling everything is spiraling out of control. It might have something to do with the big gator, lazily swimming by with a bird hitching a ride on its back. I'm also positive it's watching us out of the corner of its eye, probably sizing us up as potential dinner for later.

The bayou tour we're on is both beautiful, calming, and a little nerve-racking all at the same time. A fact not helped by the thick mist beginning to coat the trees and slither over the water. When I spot the tour guide giving the boat driver a nervous look and making a sudden excuse to turn around, my nerves heighten just that bit more.

I'm pleased to notice the others are looking about a little warily too. I know deep down it's bad to feel pleased we're all in the same boat, both literally and mentally, yet I am. I can't help it. I don't like being the only one feeling nervous.

It doesn't take us long to realize the mist is no ordinary occurrence. Magick coats it in dark tendrils, feeling its way over the bayou. A laugh of amusement with a hint of cruelty echoes around us. Like a flickering whip, it lashes forward before retreating.

A snarl of aggravation curls my lips, and I ease out tendrils of my own power, hunting the source of the magick in the mist. I sense the others around me are prepared to attack the unknown given the opportunity. What was a peaceful trip has begun to turn into what feels like a supernatural pissing match. Not good.

"Can you tell anything about the magick user?" Victor quietly growls into my ear, causing shivers of desire to ripple through me. Mentally, I chastise my hormones. After all, talk about bad timing!

"No, well, except…"

"Except what?"

"It has a weird texture to it. It's hard to explain. It's almost as if it's…" Shaking my head, I look to Felicity and T.T. to see if they can sense or explain what I'm getting from the magick. Receiving shrugs and uncertain looks, I try again to explain what it feels like.

"It's like a kid playing with chemicals, throwing different ones into a pot just to see what will happen. To me, that is what this magick feels like, a complete mess and experiment; just wrong."

I hear a whimper and glance toward the source. Our boat driver and tour guide look like they're about to have a nervous breakdown, or at the very least throw us all overboard and flee for their lives.

Once more, the laughter flows forward from somewhere in the mist. This time though it holds a note of anger within its tone.

Quickly, I pulse out another wave of magick. This time I feel it surround a mass. In the distance, violet power crackles and hisses, as my magick connects with the other.

A curse rends the silence, followed by a loud crack.

Next thing I know, my magick tendrils are springing back to me. Whatever they'd held literally wrenched themselves free.

A moment later, the repressive mist lifts, vanishing as quickly as it appeared. A frog croaks nearby, breaking the silence. I notice the tour guide giving me a weird look and wonder if he's thinking of throwing us all overboard and getting the hell out of the bayou.

Chapter 7

I'd feel offended by how quickly we're kicked off the boat, except I can't blame the nervous man for wanting to get rid of us. Still, it's not as if we'd caused the strange happenings. Talia is barely off the boat before the boatman and our guide dash past her, almost knocking her into the water, hurrying straight for a destination unknown. I'm guessing they're heading to the nearest bar, probably to regale others about their strange encounter.

"Is it ever quiet where you go?" Cedrix inquires, watching the two men scurry away.

"Most of the time. You just picked the wrong time to meet us." I'm proud of the straight face I manage to keep during my answer. It's only when I see the shocked faces around me that my laughter bubbles up, and I finally crack up. "Rarely quiet, normally not so weird." Seeing the expressions on some of the girls' faces, I look at them in puzzlement. "Well, it isn't normally this odd," I grumble.

"Sure, keep telling yourself that," Vivian replies, shaking her head at me in exasperation, before turning to Cedrix. "I'm positive trouble follows her like a bad smell."

"Hey, that's not fair. It could just as easily be following any of you!" I protest. It's only once the words have flown out of my mouth, I wish I hadn't bothered opening it in the first place. Everyone turns to stare at me before sounding like a cackling bunch of hyenas as they burst out laughing.

"Nice, very nice. Just remember, when trouble happens, you're all around at the time!" On that final note, I stalk off. It would have been a fabulous exit, if I knew where I was going.

Sadly, I manage to walk off straight for a dead end. With a groan of annoyance, I'm about to head back, when I hear a man with a deep voice talking in the building beside me. His voice comes clearly through the slightly ajar window. Hearing talk of a voodoo prince, I opt to lean against the wall and listen in.

"Apparently, he was asked to cause some group problems on the bayou. Only thing is, he didn't know they were powerful. The backlash of breaking contact threw him off his feet."

"Are you serious? Is he okay? What do you know of the group?" gasps a high-pitched voice that sounds like nails down a blackboard, making me wince.

"Not much, though two of them are meant to be locals. He'll be okay. Just stunned, to be honest. Mind you, what was he thinking of, doing a magickal attack on people he knows nothing about?"

"Foolish, foolish…Did they make it back, or did he harm them?"

"Not sure. I'm guessing the only one who got hurt, though, is…"

Hearing footsteps, I quickly hurry back down the alley. I'm gutted as I'm positive I was about to hear who the voodoo prince is and maybe even who asked him to try and harm us.

Is it all of us that were the intended victims, or just

one of us?

I peek around the corner. Finding the area empty, I exit the alley. To be honest, I'm feeling confused. *Who had I heard coming, and where did they go?* Finding the correct exit, I hurry after the others and delight in the fact that I manage to scare them, when I come up behind them.

"Where the hell did you come from?" Jasmine exclaims, placing a hand over her heart.

Giving her a cheeky grin and evil chuckle, I revel in her startled expression. Ah, the things that amuse me are small, but so worth it. "I got lost," I eventually admit, to which they all burst out laughing. When everyone has finally stopped laughing, I give them a smug smile. "I did manage to gather some information though, and I'll tell you all about it, once we're out of here," I add before indicating for them to lead the way.

"Not taking any more chances of getting lost?" chuckles Victor, from beside me.

Looking up into his beautiful silvery-green eyes, I return his smile. "Hell no, losing my way in such a small area one time is more than enough, thanks."

We follow the others back to the minivan. Climb in and buckle up. Cedrix then drives us off to destination unknown.

Chapter 8

Our destination is a little café that serves beignets and coffee. With food and drinks before us, I update everyone on what I'd overheard, ending with hearing someone coming and finding no one around.

"To be honest," I say, my voice reflecting the confusion I feel, "I'm totally unnerved by the idea of an invisible person, even more than the thought of a voodoo person trying to attack us. Which, if you think about it, is odd," I finish, scrunching up my face as I try to figure it all out.

Selecting a beignet, I take a bite of it as I look at the others in hope that they will come up with some bright idea that will solve all our problems.

"Mmm, yummy, these are gorgeous," I mutter between one bite and the next, until finally I've devoured it and lick my fingers clean.

"Glad you enjoyed it," chuckles Cedrix in apparent amusement. In the next instant, he looks and sounds serious. "I've been thinking…"

"Oh no, this could be dangerous," gasps Jezebel in mock horror. A large hand clamps across hers where it lies on the table, silencing her more effectively than anything else could.

I watch her look at the hand and then the owner of it. I can't help feel slightly in awe of Cedrix, for being able to do something as simple as place his hand over

Jezebel's, without having a reaction from her. Due to her childhood, she's always tried to limit physical contact with others, and especially men.

The look of pure peace that shines from my friend's face is wonderful and surprising. Out of the corner of my eye, I spy my sisters-in-arms, gazing in surprise and pleasure at the man who brought calmness and peace to our friend.

"Minx." Cedrix chuckles, as he looks intently into Jezebel's eyes. "Seriously though—" Tearing his gaze away, he looks around at us. A flicker of surprise crosses his features, probably due to our reactions to the simple exchange between him and our normally prickly friend.

"Umm…" Shaking his head as if to clear it, he looks at us with a slightly perplexed expression before continuing. "I was wondering if you'd mind if I brought my boss in on…well, everything that has been going on to be honest. He'll be able to help."

"Do you trust him?" I ask, even though I'm guessing his answer is yes, otherwise why would he mention his boss.

"With my life. Rob Wiseman is a friend as well as my boss. We served together in the navy SEALs."

"Then bring him up to date on the situation. If he wants to help, you can introduce us. That way, there's no pressure on him," I reply before picking up my mug of coffee and drinking a fortifying sip.

We all chill out for a while longer, just enjoying the time out. I love the atmosphere of New Orleans, the busy relaxedness of it. Even the people who are hurrying toward their destination are doing it in an unrushed way. I must admit; I'm finding it completely fascinating.

Once we've all finished eating and drinking, we climb to our feet and join the bustling crowds. We wander around, just enjoying the sights and feel of the place. Cedrix leaves us to head off to have a word with his boss, promising to catch up with us later.

I'm hoping his friend will be with him. We could do with all the help available.

"While we're on the subject of help and information—" I suddenly blurt out, startling the others.

"Uh-oh, that doesn't sound good," mutters Felicity under her breath.

Ignoring her, I carry on, refusing to make eye contact with anyone. "So I was thinking that maybe I should go back to the boat dock and search the buildings, see if I can come up with any information."

Victor strides over to me, his movements catching my eye, causing me to swallow. He moves with such power and grace, all masculine and strong, yet silently. Again, I get the impression of a fierce black panther stalking its prey. And I'm it!

Stopping directly in front of me, he places two fingers under my chin, forcing it gently yet firmly up, until I make eye contact with him.

"You're thinking about going on your own, aren't you?" he growls at me, causing shivers of desire to flicker over my skin, as his voice reverberates around me.

"Yes."

"Not happening" is his only reply—well, except for the glare he throws me.

"Actually, it is," I growl back, slapping his fingers away from me, lifting my chin higher to return his

29

glare.

His lips twitch. "How about one person goes with you? Safety in numbers, without there being too many to cause attention." He strokes the side of my face, as if he can't help himself.

"Fine, one person, and preferably a shapeshifter, just in case," I add.

****

Scuttling down the Parisian streets, I can't help glancing nervously over my shoulder. A feeling of dread and deep unease has stayed with me since fleeing Whitechapel and the Shadow World. Spying a shiver of movement in the alley beside me, I stifle a yelp of alarm.

"The boundaries are breaking. It's the only explanation. Either that or I'm being haunted by the past." Rubbing my face tiredly, I look properly into the alley. A slight breeze rustles some loose papers, lifting them and dropping them. Otherwise, all is quiet.

A feeling of exhaustion and despair washes over me, almost bringing me to my knees. Turning away, I hurry to my sister's apartment as the past assaults my memories. An image of the first man I killed flashes before my eyes. I remember being so excited, when my father informed me he was taking me on my first hunt.

I remember feeling almost giddy at the thought of righting the wrong the couple created with their blasphemous ways. After all, what right did they have to go against The Protectors, and associate with each other in such a scandalous way?

Except, when we arrived to do our duty we only found Killian Reynolds. His wife and child were out. We waited as long as we could until news came forcing us to leave. It took a further three years to find Cynthia Reynolds, and that was the first time I caught a glimpse of her daughter, Candi.

A whimper escapes me as the memories I try to keep buried once more torment me. Shame wraps around, me as guilt once more assails me. Of the thousands I'd been sent to kill, her parents' deaths are the only ones I regret.

Her heartbroken cries upon finding her mother echo in my memory. I'd watched her, remembered her broken cry of "not again," as she fell to her knees in anguish and despair. Saw her reach for her mother with trembling hands, her long red hair loose around her shoulders, and despair and pain etch into her beautiful face as tears streamed down it.

Deep in my frozen heart, I knew those cries were also for her father. That she had found both her parents, murdered by my father's and my hands. In the space of three years we'd destroyed her life. Yet she thrived, became powerful beyond belief, and now she would be sentenced to death...

Chapter 9

Night had fallen, and Jezebel and I are staking out the warehouses around the dock area we were at earlier. She's prattling on about something, and I can't for the life of me figure out what it is.

"Will you stop with the abbreviations. It takes me too long to decipher what you're trying to say. Just say it!" I finally hiss at her in frustration.

"It's meant to save time," she grumbles back at me, as she narrows her eyes in annoyance.

"O.F.," I mutter back, looking slightly over her left shoulder.

"What?"

"O.F. as in 'Oh Fuck' we've been spotted," I reply with a groan as I stare up at a tank of a man striding toward us. I mean seriously, he's huge, both in height and width. I'm positive his muscles have muscles.

Jezebel, ever so slowly turns around to face the fast-moving man, I hear a gulp and a "holy fucking hell" coming out on the barest breath of a whisper as she scoots backward toward me.

"What are you two doing here?" demands a high-pitched voice. My brain stutters in surprise as it tries to make the connection between the man and the voice.

"Say what?" mutters Jezebel in shock, turning to look at me with widening eyes, a hint of devilish amusement sparking to life in her expression.

"Don't do anything we'll both regret. He's still humongous," I mutter back. "We were out for a run, and stopped to…um, rest for a second," I reply. I have no idea how I thought my lame ass excuse would help, especially when it doesn't sound convincing even to me!

"Uh huh, a run. Shouldn't you be wearing jogging clothes?"

Climbing to our feet, we step back so as not to strain our necks as we look up at all six foot eight inches of towering muscle.

"Normally, we do. It was a spontaneous idea," Jezebel adds with a grimace.

"Right. Maybe you should both come with me." He reaches out as if to grab us. We bounce out of his way before his plate-size hands can come in contact with us.

"What the hell do you think you're doing?" I demand as I dodge his grasping hands.

"You two need to come with me. Now stay still!" whines the formidable giant.

"Sorry, not happening. We were told to never go anywhere with strangers," splutters Jezebel, trying to control her amusement.

"Oh, well, I'm Archibald Dight. Apparently, my great, great, I'm not sure how many greats, couldn't pronounce his R's and our name was written down as Dight instead of Right," Archibald bemoans to our utter bafflement.

"Okay, why are you telling us this?" I ask, feeling utterly perplexed, as I pause for a split second to gape at him.

"Because now I'm not a stranger, and you can come with me," he replies, taking another swipe at us.

This time though he manages to grab my shoulder in a bruising grip. I feel a snarl of rage curl my lips. Gathering power, I lash out at him, hitting him squarely in the chest. His hand wrenches from me as he flies back a couple of feet.

Without looking back, Jezebel and I turn around and flee into the underbrush, heading to where we'd left a rucksack hidden between some trees on the other side of the road.

Jezebel quickly strips and transforms into her jaguar form, while I put her shoes and clothes into the backpack, before putting it on my back. I then transform into wolf form, and together we slink away, keeping to the denser underbrush and trees.

After a short distance, we crouch down and watch Archibald crash through the area on the opposite side of the road. He's making enough noise to wake the dead and a sleepy-looking man exiting one of the buildings.

"What are you doing?" he demands around a huge yawn.

"I'm trying to find them girls."

"What girls? And why would you think they would be hiding in the underbrush that I can see from here is too short to cover anything bigger than a housecat?" demands the now more alert-looking man as he glances around the area.

"The ones I think the True Prince is after," whines Archibald, while swiping his arms through the high grass.

True Prince? What is the True Prince, a Prince of?

"Then search in high grass, for fuck's sake. Find them, for we won't hear the last of it if we let them slip through our fingers!" declares the other man in a voice of such determination, I know we need to get away now, or we won't be going anywhere.

Jezebel and I flatten ourselves against the ground, as we watch the man scan the area. *Obviously, he's the brains of the pair.* Easing our way backward, we creep away, when at a far enough distance we clamber to our paws and dash away, heading for Jezebel's car which we'd parked a couple of streets away, just in case of an emergency.

Before we arrive, I transform back into my human form and casually walk to the car with a large black jaguar pacing beside me.

Chapter 10

By the time we've rejoined the others, I'm feeling more puzzled by the oddity of the encounter with Archibald Dight, than anything else. Part of me wishes I'd gone with him, to see if I would have learned anything, yet the thought of doing so gives me the heebie-jeebies.

I'm also wondering who the other guy is, and why they were there, especially when everything was closed. None of it makes any sense.

We quickly update the others on our bizarre stakeout, to which we get a couple of snickers when I mention the introduction-so-we-would-go-with-him part.

"Seriously? He introduced himself and gave a little family history, thinking that would make you two go with him?" giggles T.T. in amusement.

"Yeah, he did. It was all so…surreal," Jezebel replies, looking completely baffled.

"Weird, I'm guessing he's not all there," Vivian adds, looking thoughtfully at Jezebel and I, as if this will give her the answers she's after.

"Actually, I disagree." Shaking my head, I feel as shocked as the others look by my declaration. At the same time, now that I'm thinking about it, maybe I am on the right track.

"Why do you say that?" Victor, looks at me

thoughtfully, leaning casually against the kitchen counter, arms and ankles crossed, a pose of undeniable strength.

"I'm not sure, to be honest," I reply, shaking my head as if the movement can shake my thoughts into order. "It's just a feeling and…"

"And…?" asks Victor quietly, yet with a world of intensity in his voice and eyes.

Shaking my head, I admit, "I honestly don't know. It's just something…doesn't add up about the whole scenario." Thinking about it, I try to think of what caused the iffy feelings about Archibald.

"Because of his size and magickal signature, he kind of reminded me a little of Big Michael…but there was something wrong, almost devious about Archibald," I finally say slowly, while thinking about the two giant men.

"Who the hell is Big Michael?" demands Nancy in confusion.

"He's a friend and colleague of mine, helps with demon situations, mainly extracting information from them," answers Victor while staring intently at me.

"Demons…they're real?" exclaims Selena in shock.

Nodding my head, I turn to look at Selena. "Yes, they are. Which reminds me, Victor, is there any news on my grandmother's demon impersonator?"

"Your what?" laughs Janna, in genuine amusement, until she sees my serious expression. "Are you being serious?"

At the same time, Victor answers, "Nothing yet. I must ring him and ask."

"Sadly, yes, I am," I reply. "Being serious," I

clarify when I receive blank stares from Janna and a couple others.

"Holy cow, who would have guessed?" mutters Vincent in confusion.

"Strangely enough," chuckles Jasmine, "that's exactly what we thought when we found out vampires were real."

For some reason, I find this comment extremely funny. Maybe it's because two vampires are in the room, one of which I'm sleeping with. Or my poor brain just needs a lighter moment after everything that has happened over the last few months.

What with returning home to Paradise Falls, finding a dead body, meeting Kheda and Victor, solving more murders, then Victor's bar being blown up, my grandmother going bad, which still sounds strange just thinking about it.

Hunting for the Prophecy and finding an entrance into the Shadow World. Disappearing and ending up in the past and back again, including one time butt naked! And if all that wasn't enough, we then found the Daphmire Janna and Vincent, Victor's childhood best friend and vampire brother, and rescued Roísín. Yeah, a good laugh is just what I need.

I can't help it; I burst out laughing and can't stop, even when I have tears running down my face and a stitch in my side.

Thankfully, the others seem to find the comment just as funny, either that or me gasping like a fish out of water sets them off. Though it could also be the release of the past stress affecting them too.

Cedrix arrives, and upon seeing us all in different stages of laughter, he looks slightly perplexed. I wonder why he looks worried between gasping for air and catch sight of a large man following him into the kitchen.

Finally, we slowly gain control of ourselves. Wiping tears of laughter from my face, I gain enough control to admit, "I needed that. I feel so much better now."

"I gather from what little Cedrix told me you've all had a stressful time. By the looks of you all, you really did need that laugh." Strolling into the kitchen, the man looks at all of us, assessing each one of us in a couple of seconds.

His voice surprises me, as the deep bass has an almost honey texture to it. Soothing yet firm, instilling confidence yet at the same time, it has a do-not-fuck-with-me tone ringing loud and clear through it.

Standing straight, I look at him carefully. He's at least six foot three with ebony skin that encases well defined muscles. Wearing faded blue jeans and a plain V-neck t-shirt, he looks relaxed, yet his no-nonsense steel-capped boots let me know that he's ready for anything. Well, that and his navy-blue eyes and predatory walk. This is a man who can handle himself and probably any situation thrown at him.

"Yes, we have," I answer his question. "So, Rob Wiseman, may I call you Rob? What exactly has Cedrix told you about us and what's been happening?"

"You may call me Rob, and nothing specific. Cedrix only asked me to come and meet you all, and informed me it would be best if one of you explained the situation."

"You would make an excellent poker player; you give hardly anything away," I reply with a slight growl, "Now, once more, what were you told, and please, I can sense the lie, so don't do it again!" The final words come out on a snarl, causing the man in front of me to widen his eyes slightly. I'm guessing he's surprised that I knew he lied to me. What I can't understand, though, was why he did.

Chapter 11

An hour later, we've explained to Rob everything, from finding the first body in Paradise Falls, leading Jasmine and I to meet Kheda and Victor, where we solved some murders, before being sent on a quest to England, Romania, and finally America.

How we rescued Roísín, and freed the other supernatural being held captive and tortured by the humans. And finally, about the growing war between *The Protectors* and the supernaturals who dare to have a relationship with others of a different magickal race. Supernaturals just like my parents, who were murdered by *The Protectors*.

Sitting on the sofa in the sitting room, I notice Rob is looking a little shell-shocked, to say the least. Mind you, with everything he's just found out, it isn't too surprising, and to be honest, he's handling it rather well.

"Holy shit..." Rob finally mutters, trailing off he looks around at us, opens and closes his mouth a couple of times before swallowing and trying again, "Are you serious?" Looking around again, he reaches a shaking hand toward his coffee mug on the table in front of him, before pulling his hand back as if he burnt it on the mug he never touched.

"Yes, we're serious," I soothingly reply, feeling like I'm trying not to spook a nervous horse that is ready to bolt. I look at the others in hope someone will take over. I don't quite know what to say.

"I know how this all sounds, trust me," Cedrix suddenly says. "It wasn't that long ago that I had the crash course in the supernatural war that's going on. I need you to come to terms with this. It's real, and it's happening. We need your help," he finishes in the bluntest tone I've heard in a while.

"What I want to know is why you think this is my problem? Don't get me wrong," Rob informs us, glancing at each of us in turn. "I get you're all in a difficult and dangerous situation. I'm human, though, so it doesn't affect me."

"You're right," I agree, "for the moment it doesn't, but I'm not sure how long that will be the case. The people who held Roísín and the others captive, they were human too. *The Protectors* are recruiting humans, which means it won't be long before this war spills into everyone's homes, no matter if they're supernatural or not, or even if they want in on the fight."

I watch Rob staring intently at Cedrix until, with a final look at all of us, he gives a slight nod of agreement. Determination seeps into his face, and his back becomes straighter as his shoulders uncurl from their hunched position. I'm glad to have him on our side, as I'm positive he would make a formidable enemy.

Tension seeps out of the room as everyone exhales in relief. I have no idea what we would have done if Rob hadn't agreed to help us. I'm just glad he has. After all, we need all the help we can get. Failing is so not an option.

"So what now?" Jasmine asks, glancing between

all of us with a determined expression on her face. An expression I notice the others have too.

We're all getting mentally ready for the battle coming. I only wish it could be avoided.

"I think we should contact the rest of our old unit," Cedrix informs Rob. He waits a split second for a firm nod of agreement from him before continuing, "They know how to fight and are definitely good to have on our side."

"If you think they'll help, then call them. Before you do, though, Rob, who were you thinking of that made you pause before agreeing?" I ask turning to stare intently at him while sending out tendrils of power to poke his aura. "If you have any doubts about asking someone, say so. We can't have uncertainty on members of a team joining us. After all, our lives will depend on each other defending one another's backs."

"You're right. Jacob Calico is who I have doubts about." Putting a large hand up in the air to stop any interruptions, he continues, "Cedrix, do you remember how he acted toward women and anyone with the slightest difference about them? Even you with your intuition caused him to react badly, almost…"

"As if he would happily throw me in a pit and walk away," Cedrix quietly answers while rubbing the side of his forehead with two fingers, as if to rub away or bring forth a distant memory.

"Exactly, and he only stopped acting that way when you saved his neck. Personally, I don't think it's wise to bring him into this group and have him act that way until each of them gets a chance to save his ass, so he'll trust them." I watch Rob shake his head with a look of mild exasperation, and the tiniest hint of wiry amusement twists his lips in an upward direction.

"Only call those that you both agree on," I instruct them, before standing and pacing over to the window to stare out into the night. *So much is happening, so many decisions to make that affect so many unknown people. I hope we make the right choices; after all, we'll only have one shot at this.*

I drag my fingers through my hair, giving it a slight tug to release some of the tension building inside of me. When large strong hands land on my shoulders, dig in, and massage them, I can't help leaning backward into the strength of the vampire who stole my heart, as a groan of contentment escapes me.

A feather-light kiss lands on top of my head, before the chocolate decadence of his rich voice rumbles through his big body and whispers into my ear, "What do you need, my love? Tell me, and I'll make it happen."

"I need—I need to go to the graveyard," I reply, surprising myself of the certainty and desperate need suddenly vibrating through me.

"What? Now?" Victor turns me to face him.

"Yep, apparently, right now. Go figure, because I sure as hell can't figure out the sudden urgency practically screaming through me," I mutter in reply, just before transforming into my wolf and dashing from the room. I vaguely hear a startled gasp and assume it's from Rob—after all, he's the only one that hasn't seen any of us transform before—and shouts of, "What's going on?" as I dash into the kitchen and out the large dog flap.

Jezebel must have had it especially made to allow her jaguar in and out, is my only thought before I dart

44

through it. Hugging the trees and keeping to the shadows, I race through the streets toward the cemetery. I hear noises from behind me and wonder if the others are following. Before long, I'm approaching the gates and speed up to jump onto the nearest wall and scramble over.

Urgency races through me, making me scurry around the tombs in a breakneck speed until finally I reach Marie Laveau's resting place, where a group of colorfully robed people are casting a spell. Sensing malevolence, I transform into my human form, casting a spell as I go. My wolf shape slides from me as a ball of violet magick crackles and grows swirling around me.

I feel my hair blow backward in a nonexistent wind and sense the presence of Jasmine in her Alsatian form and Victor coming up beside her.

Jezebel in her jaguar form stalks forward, flanked either side by Kheda and Vivian in their werewolf forms. Bringing up the rear are Felicity and T.T. who are already casting spells, and Janna, with her sword, though I have no idea where the hell she pulled it from. The only time I've seen it before was when I travelled back in time and saw her fighting.

"You?" hisses a male, whom I'm guessing is the leader of the group. The others are gathered around him and directing their energy into him. "You dare to disturb me with your unnatural magick?"

"Say what? There is nothing unnatural about my magick, you pompous ass," I growl back. I mean, seriously, what the hell? I watch in slight amusement as he splutters in shock. Going by his reaction, you'd swear no one had ever called him one before.

"Silence!" Spittle flies from his mouth as he waves his arms about in a rather demented fashion, right before he fires a spell at me.

Chapter 12

My ball of fire bleeds outward and around my group, encircling us in a wall of protection, so when the pissed-off twit's spell is fired, all it does is bounce off my protection shield and splutter out onto the ground.

I'm surprised when I hear the group in front of me draw in a harsh breath as if they're one entity, shocked by the sudden turn of events. Ignoring them, I let my power expand, stretch, and feel out the darkness that had me racing here in the first place.

My magick encircles and prods at the shadows surrounding us until finally it wraps around an entity, latching tentively onto it and dragging it toward me. With a vicious wrench, it breaks free and darts away with a cackle of laughter echoing in the stillness.

"What was that?" demands Janna from behind me. When I turn to her, she looks surprisingly spooked. I've never seen her look anything other than in complete control or worried.

"I'm not sure. Nothing good though. Whatever it was, it is what I sensed earlier," I reply, turning back to face the others. "Did you call it?" I demand, narrowing my eyes at them and baring my teeth in an aggressive warning.

Shaking his head in denial, the leader of the group splutters out a no, while doing a magnificent impression of a wide-eyed startled rabbit caught in the headlights, with nowhere to run.

"Who are you?"

Straightening his shoulders and raising his chin, he proclaims in a self-important voice, "I am the Voodoo Prince Jayden, descended from the Voodoo Queen Marie Laveau."

"Ugh huh, what the fuck were you doing?" I growl back. *Please tell me you at least knew what you were doing* I silently beg.

"Calling forth Marie, of course," replies a woman from behind Jayden, as if it's obvious.

"Yeah, I have this strange feeling you fucked it up, because whatever that was," I inform them, pointing in the general direction of where the entity disappeared, "it wasn't Marie Laveau. It was something…other," I reply, as a trickle of unease slithers down my spine. *What the hell was it?*

"How do you know it wasn't Marie?" inquires another robed woman stepping forward and waving a hand behind her at the tomb.

"Because, whatever that was, was never alive in this plane before," I reply, staring at each of them in turn, while wishing they'd remove their hoods. "It was something old and dangerous. I'd advise you to remember exactly what spell you cast, and exactly how you did it. It's the only hope you'll have of catching and returning it to wherever it came from."

I turn away from them, pause, and turn back to throw one final comment their way. "Oh, and the sooner you do it the better. It'll be hungry soon, and I'm guessing whatever it eats won't be a burger." As one, my group heads back the way we came, no one says anything. All I know though is, I can't wait to leave this gorgeous city.

"Wait!" hollers a scared-sounding Voodoo Prince, "Please, we need your help."

A groan of exasperation eases from me as I turn back to face him.

"I don't know how to get rid of it," he mutters. "We need help, and apparently, you seem to know what you're doing."

"Ugh. You have got to be kidding me," I mutter in exasperation.

"We gotta help," pipes up Jezebel. "I love it here and don't fancy it being destroyed if we can help it."

"I know you're right," I agree, feeling completely exhausted and wondering what the hell we can do that this group can't, when a thought pops into my head. Turning to Jayden, I ask the question center in my mind, "Who is your necromancer?"

"My necromancer...? Well, umm, yeah, we don't have one. It's not as if we're raising the dead just..."

"What?" I shout, causing everyone around me to jump, from the sudden loudness in the otherwise silent night. "What the hell do you mean, you don't have a necromancer?" Sparks crackle to life, flickering around my fingers and racing up my arms.

"We weren't raising anyone from the dead, just..." stammers someone from the group of idiots before me.

"Calling spirits, speaking to them, or raising them from the dead all need a necromancer to make sure you have control and are calling the right one forward. Otherwise, you can get anyone or thing answering and entering the void," I thunder at them, as fury encompasses me. *How can they have been so stupid?*

I can feel the color in my face bleed away as fear

49

settles inside me. Turning to Victor, I say the only thing that bounces around my skull. "Can you please get Selene and Nancy and bring them both here?"

He rubs his hands soothingly up and down my arms, easing the turmoil swirling around me. "I'll be right back," he informs me before flitting away.

I turn back toward the group as a ferocious growl rumbles through it, causing the cloaked figures to look nervously at each other and scramble backward in a rather creepy tumble, reminding me of large beetles. I can't stand bugs. They give me a bad case of the heebie-jeebies.

"Candi, calm down," mutters T.T, as she steps closer to my right side and grasps hold of my hand, giving it a reassuring squeeze.

Taking a deep breath, I hold it, count to ten, and release it. The fifth time of inhaling, holding, and releasing, I finally feel myself calm enough to talk. Closing my eyes, I let my magick search the surrounding air, seeking anything that either might help or at the very least might try and hinder us on our search for capturing the entity.

To be honest, I'm not sure if I'm relieved or disappointed when I find nothing except a distant trace of the path it took, almost as if it left a footprint in the air. Something I've never felt before.

Turning to T.T. and Felicity, I ask them if they have ever sensed such footprints and receive blank stares for my trouble. Guessing that means no, I ask them to sense the ether and find them. After all, this could be very handy in tracking.

"I can't find them," T.T. replies five minutes later, rubbing the furrow marks in her forehead with her fingertips. The way she was frowning in concentration, I wouldn't be surprised if she gave herself a headache!

"Me neither," admits Felicity a moment later, shaking her head in frustration. "It must be another talent that's just yours," she adds, shrugging her shoulders while a grimace pulls her full lips down. "I gotta admit; I'm feeling a tiny bit jealous of your new abilities."

"Me too," pipes up T.T., giving me a shrug of her shoulders when I turn to gape at her.

"What, why?" Looking between the two of them, I feel surprise at their admission. Not because they admitted it, as we have a habit of saying what we think or feel to one another; it's more of the fact that they feel that way that confuses me.

"Don't worry; we'll get over it," Felicity reassures me. "It's just you always were different with kickass magick and—"

"It can be hard to see how much further you've progressed, while we haven't," T.T. interrupts to add. "Don't get us wrong, though; I'm excited for you. I just wish we had the abilities too."

"Exactly," Felicity agrees with a grin spreading across her face.

Before anything else can be said, Victor, Nancy, and Selena arrive. The moment Selena stands in front of the tomb, she stiffens. "What the hell happened here?" she demands with a trace of fury lacing her voice.

"Ah crap, it must be worse than we thought!" is the only thing I manage to exclaim in reply.

Chapter 13

"Does a bear shit in the woods?" is Nancy's unhelpful reply, making me feel slightly baffled.

"Umm, yeah, is this a trick question, because I don't see the connection?" T.T. replies, staring in confusion at Nancy.

"I'm glad I'm not the only one feeling confused," I mutter to her, only to receive a relieved look back.

"No, it's not a trick question," Nancy replies, giving us both a look of wry amusement. "I only meant you were stating the obvious. This whole situation is a major clusterfuck, if ever I saw one."

"Ahh, okay. Why the hell didn't you just say that?" I demand before raising a hand to stop any further comment. "Never mind, it doesn't matter."

"What exactly happened here?" Selena asks, staring at each of us as if we've all grown a couple of extra heads each.

We haven't. I know this because I check. Can't help it, pure instinct takes over. Apparently, I wasn't discreet, for I hear a couple of groans and a distinctively delicious male chuckle.

"Don't worry, there's still only one beautiful head on your shoulders," Victor informs from directly behind me, as he caresses the back of my neck, causing an instant ripple of desire to ripple through my body.

"They fucked up." Felicity points at the group in

front of us, just to make sure who "they" are is understood.

"All right, who are you, and what the hell were you trying to do?" Selena growls at the cowering group.

"I am the Voodoo Prince Jayden, and these"— Jayden waves a hand about indicating the people in his group—"are my followers."

"Right…I wouldn't go declaring yourself a Voodoo Prince if I were you. It gives the impression you know what you're doing and are the best at it," Selena bluntly informs him. Taking a moment to loosen her muscles, mainly by shaking her hands and rotating her head, she closes her eyes and suddenly goes still.

"What is she doing?" demands Jayden, sounding slightly worried and curious at the same time.

"Preparing to get to work," I reply, glancing at him for a split second before turning my gaze back to my friend.

A second later, Selena gives a barely noticeable nod, before folding herself into a sitting position in front of Marie Laveau's crypt, resting her hands flat on the ground either side of her crossed legs.

Nancy steps up behind her, placing both her hands on her shoulders, while T.T., Felicity, and I stand behind Nancy, clasp hands with one another and raise a circle of protection around us and the tomb.

Power flares to life, the ground shakes, and everything goes deathly quiet.

"I call on you, Marie Laveau, to come forth and help us on our quest," Selena calls out. *"I call on you to help find and return the entity released by your descendent Jayden."*

"I'm a Voodoo Prince," mutters Jayden in

annoyance, which everyone ignores.

"I call on you, as a necromancer of the first order of Helios, descended from Margaret Holden, of the necromancer's Holden line."

A colorfully dressed woman steps from the dark shadows of the burial site into our circle.

One of the first things I notice is the strength of her character shining through. This woman is powerful. She has gorgeous caramel skin and beautiful ebony eyes, and a turban covers her hair. Full lips turn slightly upward in a partial smile, though her gaze is assessing and filled with curiosity.

When she finally speaks, her accented voice sounds like honey wrapped in sugar, beautiful to listen to, yet it's the command in her tone that catches my attention.

"Now who are you, and why have you disturbed me?" Marie Laveau asks, stepping directly in front of Selena.

"I am your descendant, Voodoo Prince Jayden..."

"You are no Voodoo Prince; my magick don't be part of you. I'm not even sure if we be related, boy. Though you do look a bit like my cousin," Marie grudgingly informs him, before turning away, effectively dismissing him.

"I am Selena. I am the one who called you," Selena says, before Jayden or any of his followers can utter another word. The rest of us allow Selena to be spokesperson. After all, she is the necromancer and unless any of us are directly spoken to, it's best to stay quiet.

"I have called you to ask for your help in fixing"— turning to look at Jayden, she points at him—"his blunder. Apparently, he tried to call you forth and instead released an entity of unknown name or origins."

Sudden stillness takes hold of Marie. "You released the demon Solomon?" she roars in fury, scaring the crap out of me at her sudden volume.

Solomon, as in King Solomon, was he a demon? I thought the story was he captured the fallen angels?

"I'm sorry, Solomon who?" Selena asks, sounding just as shocked as I'm feeling.

"You be knowing the one. I can see it in your eyes. Yes, he be a demon of the first order and captured the angels who fell. Imprisoned them and almost created hell on earth. That part of the story everyone left out."

"How can we stop him? Send him back to…"

"You can't. You need to track him to capture him, and he's gone!"

"What if we have a way to track him? Will you help us capture him?" demands Selena, with a hint of hope in her voice.

"It takes a unique magick to track…" She pauses to look once more at us. Her brow furrows as she smells the air around us, her eyes flickering between our group, once more taking us all in. "If you can track him, I'll help you," she finally agrees.

Chapter 14

I feel the tension in my shoulders loosen. Deep down, I know we can't get rid of Solomon without her help. Though at the same time, I wonder how much of what she's told is the truth. Is the entity really Solomon from the Bible, or is it something else entirely?

I sense she believes what she said, yet something about what I felt and have been told isn't aligning within me. Reminding me of the game Chinese Whispers. By the time the story goes around, it's changed drastically, though still holds a tiny bit of the original.

I turn to look at a dejected-looking self-proclaimed Voodoo Prince. He'd believed he was directly linked to Marie. He'd believed to such an extent that he landed himself and us in this mess. Yet one look at him, and the Voodoo Queen knew he was only distantly related to her.

So, who had told him they were related by a closer blood link?

"Jayden, who told you about your relationship to Marie, and what made you think it made you a Voodoo Prince?" I finally ask, as there's no point wondering when I haven't the answers.

"My mother told me." His answer comes out in such a sullen voice I almost laugh.

Seriously, is he sulking?

"So, let me get this straight; your mum told you were related the Voodoo Queen, and what, you declared yourself a prince?"

"No," Jayden hotly denies. "My mother told me we are directly descended from her, and that I am the next Voodoo Prince."

"Well, your mama lied to you. You are not directly descended from me and are most definitely not a prince..." Marie Laveau denies, with a swipe of her hand through the air as if to empathize her point.

"But she showed me the family tree," Jayden shouts at Marie, sounding and looking as if he's about to burst into tears.

*I'm beginning to wonder if he was accidentally swapped at birth. Maybe with a distant cousin...*I turn to look at Jezebel. One thought bounces around my head, and I wonder if she's thinking the same thing. When my eyes connect with hers, she gives her head a nod.

Could he be the True Prince that Archibald and the other man were on about? Holy shit!

"Enough." Swiping her hand through the air, Marie effectively stops any further comments. "I don't care what you were told or seen, your blood says it all. The point be your ineptitude at spell-casting, not your blood!"

Turning to Selena, she stares at her for a moment before once more looking at the rest of us, as if searching for something. "How do you plan on tracking?"

"Candi caught his trail. We're hoping she can catch it again and follow it," Selena replies from where she's still sitting on the ground.

"Once you find his trail and have tracked him, call me, and I will come."

"How do we catch him?"

"You don't, necromancer; that be my job. You call me from wherever you are when you find him. Just take a bit of the soil here, and I will come."

A second later, she turns and walks back into her tomb. Selena closes the connection, and T.T., Felicity, and I pull our magick back into ourselves, releasing the protective circle.

"Well, that was different," Nancy mutters. She waits while her sister collects some soil and ties it into a handkerchief and then helps her up. Once Selena is standing, she turns around to face the rest of us. "So, how do we proceed from here? Do you think you can track it, Candi?"

"I think so," I reply, frowning, as I ponder the feeling of the connection. A shudder slithers down my back, as if icy fingers are trailing patterns over it, as I remember the way the entity felt.

Turning to the group that brought us here, I ask the question that had filtered through my head. "Who is your cousin that was born the same day as you, and does he live on the bayou?"

Profound silence greets my question, as Jayden does a wonderful impression of a fish out of water, gasping for air. Just when I thought I'd rendered him mute, he finally answers. "How do you know my cousin lives on the bayou, was born the same day as me, and is a male?" he demands in a slightly strangled tone.

"Because I'm a genius," I answer with the straightest expression I can manage. It doesn't last long as a grin escapes. "Only messing, I'm not. A simple matter of deduction really."

"Apparently, not that simple," mutters Victor from directly behind me. I turn around to look at him and can't help the warm feeling that spreads through me at the sight of him. *Damn, I've got it bad.*

"Oh, right." Suddenly realizing that the only one who probably deduced the same reasoning I did is currently a jaguar so isn't talking, I quickly explain my reasoning. "Well, when we were on the bayou earlier, someone with untrained power tried to attack us. When I was on the dock, I overheard a couple of people talking about a Voodoo Prince. Later, when Jezebel and I went back, we heard about a True Voodoo Prince. It probably was the same people, now I think about it..."

"Wait, I didn't attack anyone on the bayou. In fact, I rarely go there," exclaims Jayden in annoyance.

"Uh-huh, I didn't think it was you. Marie also said that you weren't from her direct bloodline, though you have her blood in you, just more distant..."

"I've already told you..." Jayden interrupts me once more.

"Would you let me finish," I growl at him, turning quickly to face him and flashing some fang.

"Shit, her eyes just turned violet," someone from his group mutters.

With a huh of annoyance, I continue, "With everything that has been said, it sounds like you were swapped at birth with your cousin, who I'm presuming was male and born on the same day and place as you?"

"Yes, he was," Jayden finally whispers, as his shoulders hunch in on himself.

I wonder if he'd guessed that his cousin is the true

Voodoo Prince. He must have been able to tell who was more powerful.

"My uncle was always so happy to see me…"

"I think you all need to have a little chat. Find out the truth," I quietly say, feeling just a little guilty at my part in the bombshell that has turned into his world.

"Yes. Yes, I think you're right, though why…"

"Any questions you have, your family, all of them will be able to answer," Selena reassures the dejected-looking man, who suddenly seems very young and unsure of everything.

With a nod and slight motion of his hand, he indicates to his group it's time for them to go. Turning around, he takes one step away from us before pausing and turning back. "I'm sorry for causing this…" Looking uncertainly around as if searching for a word, he finally says, "Mess, for lack of a better word," before turning around and walking off into the shadows of the surrounding tombs.

Chapter 15

Exhaustion ripples through me, and I feel myself sag. Strong arms circle my waist from behind and pull me back into a firm chest, holding me strongly against him.

"I do believe we should all go and get some sleep. Finding this entity will be best left for tomorrow when everyone is more awake and at their strongest," Victor informs us, before shifting me slightly so he can pick me up, looping one arm around my back and the other under my legs.

I do what any strong-willed knackered woman does. I fling an arm around his neck and snuggle into him, gifting him the pleasure of carrying me, while I take the opportunity to rest. I feel a fleeting kiss brush the top of my head right before darkness claims me.

****

"Sophie, I'm telling you she is the one!" I shout at my pacing sister, wishing she would stay still and just listen to me.

"She can't be. I refuse to believe this ridiculous war brought on by your fanatical group can..."

"Can what?" I ask in a tone as tired as I feel.

"Can have merit. What does it mean, what possible difference can she bring to the world?" Confusion and wonderment battle in equal measure across my sister's expressive face, while a hint of fear resonates in her

voice.

"I don't know, to be honest," I admit. My sister comes to a screeching halt and stands there swaying back and forth for a second while she gapes at me.

"You don't know? How is that even possible? You and Father hunted and murdered—"

"Executed," I interrupt, frowning at my impertinent sister. After all, she knows I was only doing my job.

"Murdered," she growls at me in such a furious tone while glaring daggers at me, I actually feel concerned she might attempt to harm me.

"You are a murderer, and you murdered them!" she bluntly informs me, standing with her hands firmly on her hips and a fierce expression I never thought she was capable of on her face. "So don't pretend the fact that it's your job changes the name of what you are or did!"

"You're right."

"What?"

"I said you're right. Don't make me repeat myself, Sophie, because I won't." I can't help the little half smile that flitters across my face for a split second. After all, it's not often I render my sister speechless.

****

I feel myself fly out of my body, where for a split-second I hover over Victor, who is about to cross over the threshold of Jezebel's door with me firmly in his arms. The others, I notice, have either already entered or are about to enter her house.

I know I'm dreaming, or at least I think I am. Just in case, I whisper a spell of protection over my body.

Let none other than I enter my body.

Keep me safe; keep me linked,
Let no harm come to my spirit or form.

The next thing I know I'm flying through the inky black sky, lit by sparkling stars, heading straight back to the cemetery. Once over the tombs, I fly in a vertical line until suddenly I zoom off after a faint trail of putrid green and black.

I've never seen anything like it before and would rather not see it now, never mind follow it! Apparently, I have no choice in the matter as my speed increases, shooting me through the night, making me feel like a demented comet after a...*Oh, is this the demon's trail I'm following?*

At this startling thought, I dive sideways and feel as if I'm about to lose some spiritual lunch. I'm positive I can feel my stomach somersaulting. What feels like thirty minutes later, I find myself hovering over a building on Bourbon Street. The only reason I know where I am is because I spot a sign telling me.

In confusion, I stare at the roof of the building, wondering what the hell I'm supposed to do now, as I am not in control of this...dream? *Am I dreaming, or is this actually happening?* As if my spirit form was waiting for me to ask, it suddenly decides to sink through the roof into the building.

I'm also pretty damn positive it gave me a mental gag, so my screams couldn't be heard outside of my terrified head, where they bounced like ping-pong balls on steroids.

"Calm yourself, Candi, and watch," Hecate's voice whispers in my skull, soothing me. With a gulp, I nod in understanding and take a deep shaky lungful of air. I only then remember I don't technically have any

lungs, which for some reason makes me want to laugh and eases my nerves.

Hearing squeaking and moaning, it takes me a second to realize I'm in someone's bedroom, and they're currently having sex. I don't know where to look, as the mirror facing the bed reflects the bobbing pale white ass and the stick legs embracing it, as they bounce away on the rickety bed.

Suddenly, I'm moving toward a wall. Sadly, it's the wall with the bed and frisky couple. With a shudder and an apology, my spirit self passes through them. Going by the heave-worthy squeal of completion, I do believe they liked it. As for me, I just want to go cry in a corner!

"Hecate, I do hope that's not what you wanted me to watch!"

"No child, prepare yourself, and remember what you hear." Hecate informs me with a good deal of amusement lacing her voice.

We pass quickly through the room with a single occupant in it. As if sensing something, the man looks around uneasily, before going back to the book in his hand.

Passing through his wall, we enter a room with two men in it.

My spirit form slides up the wall and into a corner, where I watch in fascination as a large muscular man, with buzz-cut military style hair, stares at a scrawny, pimpled teenager, who looks about seventeen years old, if he's lucky.

Two things grab my attention straight away. The first is the simple yet obvious matter that the man looks terrified of the kid. The second is the worrying fact that the kid has a demon lurking inside of him.

Red eyes stare with molten fire from the kid, while a putrid green and black cloud oozes from him, as if unable to contain the demon's essence inside the body. Going by the tendrils of nastiness escaping him, I recognize the demon Solomon from the cemetery.

I'm tempted to crow in delight, except for the fact I really, really don't want him to notice me.

"I can't take you. I can't leave the country. I'm sorry," the terrified man warbles in an exhausted voice, as if he's been having the same conversation for hours and doesn't believe he can hold on much longer.

"You will take me, or you will find someone who can!" Solomon hisses at the unfortunate man.

"I don't know anyone who can," the man whines while wringing his hands together.

"You have until tomorrow to find someone. Or you will take me yourself to Paradise Falls. No more excuses. Now leave me, and don't return unless you have someone who can fly me, or it is time for you to fly me to Ireland!"

I watch the man turn around, and somehow refrain from gasping out loud. Emblazoned on his cheek is what I'm presuming is the demon's mark of ownership. As he retreats quickly from the room, I float up and out of the roof.

The image of the peacock branded into the man's cheek causes a shudder to reverberate through me. If that symbol means what I think it does, then the demon isn't Solomon, the king known for being just and honorable, but the demon Adramelech.

Maybe the confusion over his name is simply because he was mentioned in *The Key of Solomon*. One of the most feared of the Kings of Hell. Crap, and he's heading straight for Paradise Falls.

Chapter 16

The journey back to my body is just as daunting as the journey away from it was. The relief I feel when I arrive above Jezebel's house is immense, though soon turns to confusion when, upon sinking into the house, I find my body surrounded by my friends and lover, who is shaking me by the shoulders.

"Maybe we should slap her face, see if that wakes her up?" a frazzled-sounding Jasmine asks.

"Candi, wake up!" Victor thunders in response giving me a harder shake. I'm positive I feel my teeth rattle. Before anything else can be done to me, I shoot into my body and sit up with a horrifying gasp of "Aghhh," making everyone around me jump, and a few of them scream in shock.

"Sorry about that." I can't help the note of glee or the big-ass grin that spreads across my face.

"Fuck's sake, talk about doing a zombie-coming-back-from-the-dead impression!" exclaims Nancy, placing a hand over her heart as if to calm it down.

I can't help the chuckle that escapes me at her declaration. After all, coming from a zombie, it is funny. Shaking my head in amusement, I slowly climb to my feet.

"What are you finding so goddamn funny?" growls Nancy in apparent frustration.

"Nothing, just a zombie calling me out on doing a

zombie impression," I reply, moving swiftly out of hitting range. At the couple of snickers I hear, the others at least find it amusing, even if they still seem to be worried.

"Funny comments aside, what happened to you? Are you okay, or do we need to get a doctor?" Victor asked, while running his hands down my body and wagging my wrists as if to make sure they still work.

"I'm fine, honest. I just had a…"

"A what?" Victor pauses long enough in his testing my limbs to stare intently at me. I take that second to gently pull my wrists from his grasp and stroke the sides of his face in a soothing way. Well, at least I thought it was soothing until he captures my hands in his firm grasp and pulls them away from him, holding them between us.

"An out-of-body experience…" I answer, sounding rather doubtful, even to me.

"Are you asking us or telling us?" Selena demands, from where she's now sitting on the sofa.

"Umm, not sure," I admit, before telling them what happened. Once I've told them everything, I suck in a deep breath and let it out, before looking at each stunned face in the room.

"Holy cow, that's not good, is it?" mutters Victor in shock.

"Umm, no, definitely not good," I reply, feeling slightly amused at his bewildered expression and question. "We'll have to try and stop him from leaving tomorrow. Failing that, we'll have to follow him back to Paradise Falls and try to gather more help."

"Well, at least we know where he is now." Standing up, Kheda walks over to the window, staring at the closed curtains, as if he can see something the rest of us can't. I glance from his back to Jasmine, who's looking at him curiously. I'm guessing she feels my stare, as she turns to look at me and gives a small shrug before turning to look at Kheda once more.

"Does anyone have any ideas on what to do next?" Jezebel asks, looking at each of us in turn.

I shake my head in response, putting my hand over my mouth to cover a huge yawn. I'm feeling exhausted and drained and would love to sleep for at least a month.

"How about we get some sleep, get up early, and meet for breakfast near the hotel where he's staying," Cedrix answers, while rubbing a large hand over his head and across the back of his neck, as if to ease tension. "Once we've slept and eaten, we should be able to come up with a plan to try and capture him."

We all readily agree to his plan. After all, we're all knackered, and chasing after a demon while on no energy is just plain daft, let alone dangerous. Everyone who's staying at Cedrix's house follows him to his truck and piles in, while the rest of us clamber up the stairs to our rooms.

I barely manage to prepare for bed and climb into it, before sleep claims me.

Chapter 17

Warm breath tickles the back of my neck, and a heavy arm is wrapped around my waist, anchoring me to a rock-solid body. A large hand cups my breast and squeezes it gently.

"Are you awake?" My voice sounds husky to my own ears because I'm still half asleep.

When I receive no answer, I wriggle around so I'm facing Victor and find him fast asleep, his mouth slightly open. I drink my fill of him and can't help to brush my fingers lightly over his high cheekbones and trace the contours of his gorgeous face.

For some reason while I stare at him, I remember the fortune teller on the street. Shaking my head slightly, I can't figure out what has made me remember her, or why I feel I must go and see if she's there.

With a frustrated groan, I disentangle myself from my vampire's embrace and crawl out of the depths of the blankets, dress, and hurry downstairs. Because I don't have a key to Jezebel's house, I transform into my wolf form, exit through the backdoor flap, and change back into my human form, before jogging off down the road in the hopes of finding her.

Forty-five minutes later, I have a beignet in one hand and a coffee in the other, and I round the corner to find the fortune teller setting up her stall.

"You're just in time," she informs me, without

looking up from what she's doing.

"You were expecting me?"

"Yes. Come, sit," she instructs me, waving an elegant hand with five or six bangles clinking on her wrist, directing me to the seat in front of her.

I quickly do as she instructs, while looking closely at her. She's dressed herself up once again as you would expect a fortune teller to look. Her eyes are darkly kohled, a bright scarf covers her hair, and she's wearing a colorful gypsy skirt and top, with a scarf tied around her waist. The style suits her, I decide; it's elaborate, slightly mystical looking, and elegant.

"Give me your hand," she requests in a soothing voice, as if expecting me to bolt at any moment. I place a hand, with my witch magick brand, palm up in her waiting hand and receive a nod of satisfaction from the woman in front of me. "Good, good. Now let me see what lies ahead of you," she mutters, while staring intently at my palm.

"War. New life and death lie in wait for you. Though not for long." Puzzlement flickers across her face, as if what she sees doesn't make any sense.

"What is confusing you?" I inquire, as a shiver slithers down my spine and a feeling of anticipation blossoms deep inside my stomach, uncurling like a flower's petals.

"A path you're on that makes no sense." She looks up from my hand to make eye contact with me. "I see so many changes, not just yours, though they are caused by you. Like a stone thrown in water, the ripples cross time and place. Changing everything."

"And this is bad?"

"That's what I find so strange, if this comes

true…" Shaking her head, she opens and closes her mouth, before once more looking down at my palm. "It's as if what was meant to be will come back into play. As if…"

"As if what?" I ask, on barely a breath of a whisper.

"You somehow heal and bring to life the missing magick in the world. Yet, the path is divided. One wrong step and everything will crumble. What I don't understand is how it is possible? Who are you that your path holds such power over all?"

I look into the fortuneteller's face and see hope and disbelief battle in her eyes. With a slight smile flickering across my mouth, I bring up my other palm and turn it around so she can see my wolf brand tattoo.

A startled gasp escapes her as she stares at my palms. "Double magick, you are the one? I always thought that was just a myth."

"All myths are based on truths; they've just been relegated into fables," I reply, before standing. I pay for my reading and wish her farewell.

Chapter 18

I return to Jezebel's house in time to wake Victor by nibbling his chin and tracing open-mouthed kisses along his torso. His hands delve into my long hair, wrapping around it and pulling me gently but firmly up until our mouths meet in a fiery kiss.

Releasing his hands from my hair, he quickly undresses me, rolling me under him and throwing my clothes onto the floor. Using his powerful legs, he pushes mine open, hooking them under his arms, while trailing kisses from my lips to my breasts, before piercing first one nipple and then the other with his fangs.

His tongue soothes my breasts and their happy points, causing sensation to tingle and pulse from my breasts down my body to my center, where a pulse of arousal hums through and gathers inside me.

My eyelids feel heavy, as if the pleasure lapping through me makes keeping them open impossible. Staring into Victor's beautiful silvery-green eyes with blue fire bleeding into them is the only thing keeping my eyes from closing. As if he silently demands, they stay open, and I can't refuse.

His large hands move over my body, squeezing and fondling me, while mine grapple his shoulders, hair, and the sheets beneath me, as his mouth moves down my torso until it reaches its destination.

His tongue plunges into my core before retreating and teasing my hooded lady, his lips clamping over it, tormenting me in a most delicious way, before releasing once more. He thrusts his tongue inside me while his fingers tease my nub.

Pleasure crashes through me as I buck beneath him, my hands gripping his hair and holding his head in place, until finally his talented tongue, teeth, lips, and fingers bring me to orgasm.

Rising above me, Victor thrusts his erection deep inside me. His mouth comes down to claim mine, swallowing my moans. I drape my legs over his shoulders while my hands move down to his withdrawing ass, only to grab it and bring him flush against me once more.

With a twist of his hips, he withdraws and thrusts into me, as if returning a sword to its sheath. Until finally with his fangs distended and his eyes shining blue fire from his passion, he roars his completion, biting into the side of my neck, as I bite into his, both of us drinking from the other, as our orgasms roll through us.

"I love you, Candi."

"And I love you too," I reply through our bite connection. As his blood slides down my throat, making me feel stronger, as my hands lazily trace the contours of his beautiful body. *"Mmm, I could stay here forever, just like this,"* I inform him before releasing his neck from my teeth and licking it clean.

"One day, my beauty, I'll keep you in bed and won't let you out for at least a week," Victor informs me, before retracting his fangs from my neck and giving the now-healed area a fleeting kiss. "Sadly

though, we have to get up and capture a demon king." A small laugh escapes him on these words, and amusement flashes in his eyes.

"Who would ever have thought that those words would be uttered from anyone's mouth, let alone being serious while saying them?" I groan, feeling slightly bewildered at how weird my life has become over the last few months. *Not that it was all peaches and cream before*…Looking at my vampire lover, I admit my life might have taken a trip down a weird and more unusual path than I'm used to, but I wouldn't change it back for anything.

I reach up and trace his features, marveling at his masculine beauty. "I am so in love with you. I never believed I'd ever meet someone I could love as much as I love you," I admit, before bringing his face down to mine and kissing him fleetingly before pushing him back so I can get up.

"I love you too, Candi. I don't think I can ever tell you how much you mean to me, and how happy you make me feel, just by being near you, never mind your admitting you love me," Victor informs me while climbing off the bed and reaching down to pick me up and letting my body slide down his until my feet are on the ground.

"We'd best get ready. I can hear the others rising, and we have an interesting day ahead of us. Hopefully, it won't be too difficult to capture the demon." I shake my head, at the rather incredulous look Victor flashes at me. "I know, I know. I'm not expecting it to be easy, far from it, in fact. I'm just hoping it won't be a complete catastrophe," I grudgingly admit, as images of this beautiful city getting pulverized flash before my eyes.

How the hell are we going to capture him without destroying everything?

Chapter 19

"So how are we going to do this?" Jasmine inquires forty-five minutes later, while we're all sitting around drinking coffee and eating breakfast at a café opposite the hotel Adramelech is staying in.

"No idea," I admit, taking a large bite of my sausage sandwich while ignoring the frown Jasmine sends my way.

"Oh, wonderful. I gather you're in a truly helpful mood, as you're giving out such wonderful ideas." Jasmine all but growls at me, causing me to stop chewing for a second to raise my eyebrows in bewilderment.

"What?" I ask, once I've swallowed my food.

"This is important and—"

"I know it's important. I just don't know how to deal with it," I interrupt my friend. "Look, Selena has the dirt to summon Marie, once we have Adramelech. What we need to do is figure out how to safely get near enough to him to summon her, without putting either ourselves or anyone else in jeopardy. And that is where I have no idea."

"Do you reckon we shouldn't do it here, in the hotel then?" Nancy asks me, while looking between me and an apprehensive-looking Jasmine.

"I'm not sure. The thing is, I don't think he'll give a hoot about killing or even destroying everything around us to get away." I nibble my thumbnail as I try to put my thoughts in order before continuing, "If we try apprehending him on the route to the airport, then there are the commuters to worry about. At the airport, you have the planes in flight, taking off and landing, and all the people to worry about."

"So how about we play it by ear?" Kheda advises, causing all of us to look at him. "I have to agree. I don't want to put others' lives in danger in the hopes of catching him. What we have on our side is the knowledge of where he's going."

Silence greets his statement as we all think on what's been said, until finally we all agree that playing it by ear is our best chance. Even if it's a nonhelpful plan, at least it's a plan, of sorts.

Decision made, everyone except Victor and I head back to the cars, leaving us to watch the hotel. Five minutes later, the man from the room next to Adramelech's exits the building, passing the man with the tattoo on his face I'd seen last night.

I nudge Victor's foot with my own and nod toward the man with the peacock tattoo on his face while picking up my coffee and drinking from it. Out of the corner of my eye, I watch Victor retrieve his phone from his pocket and press some buttons. I presume that means he's sending the others a text letting them know things are beginning to move. Kind of.

"Blimey, I'm knackered," I mutter after letting loose a huge yawn. "I badly need some sleep," I admit, rubbing a hand over my eyes before slapping my cheeks gently in an attempt to wake up.

A few minutes later, I spot Jezebel's car turning into the street. Getting up, Victor and I stroll toward it while I check windows for any sign of movement coming from the hotel across the street.

Ten minutes after buckling into our seats, we watch as a taxi pulls up in front of the building, and a scrawny teenager exits the hotel with the man who had entered earlier.

The teenager pauses by the taxi to turn his head in our direction. For just a split second, his face changes, becoming older. His eyes change into slits, and a smile breaks out across his face, flashing teeth sharp and pointy looking, in a mouth too wide for his face.

I can't help the shudder that shivers through me or the gasp that escapes me. A second later, his face changes back, and they both climb into the waiting taxi.

"Did you see that?" Jezebel demands in a shaky voice, while her hands grip the steering wheel so tightly I can hear it groaning.

"Yes," I answer, glad I'm not the only one who did.

"Fucking hell," mutters Victor, staring intently at the taxi that's about to turn the corner at the end of the street.

"Jezebel, you need to drive. We can't lose them now in case they go somewhere else before the airport," Janna informs her in a soothing voice, while looking worriedly at her daughter sitting between her and Vincent.

Next thing I know, we're speeding off after a demon in a taxi, almost knocking down a pedestrian who was unfortunate enough to try and cross the road. It doesn't take us long to catch up. It does, though, take us a couple of minutes to get Jezebel to stop speeding. After all, we want to follow them, not get arrested.

We quickly realize we're not heading toward the airport. That we are instead going in the opposite direction. Pulling out my phone, I call Selena. This could be our chance in stopping him before he leaves New Orleans, let alone the country.

"We're heading toward the bayou," Jezebel informs me. "Tell Cedrix to drive where we were yesterday on the boat trip."

Quickly, I relay what I've been told, wondering how he'll know where to go. After all, we were on the water yesterday, not exactly near any road.

Apparently, I had nothing to worry about, as soon enough I see Cedrix turning onto the road ahead of us. The road we're on is narrow and windy, more of a track than anything else. Trees surround us, and the smell of the bayou wafts through the open windows.

Looking out the window, I see the water between the trees and what looks like a large log floating past. Soon enough, we're pulling onto the side of the road and climbing out to proceed on foot.

It's only when the sound of manic cackling reaches us, I know we're near our destination. A split second later, the screaming starts, and the laughter gets louder. Peering through the trees, I'm just in time to see the demon teen rip apart an old man with his bare hands.

In an instant, Selene drops to the ground, dragging out the dirt she'd collected from Marie Laveau's tomb and starts chanting. Nancy places her hand on her shoulders, and the power around them intensifies.

T.T., Felicity, and I step in front of them, join hands and start chanting our own spell, one to protect us from being noticed, especially from the demon currently ripping through the people of the bayou while calling out for the Voodoo Prince to show himself.

Violet power rolls and crackles up my arms, expanding outward, while a pale yellow ripples over T.T. and Felicity, before joining mine and expanding outward. In the distance, I sense the untrained power from yesterday on the bayou coming closer, and soon blue sparks flash and writhe ahead of us, before reaching out and joining our power and connecting.

Sparks fly, before our magicks link, surrounding everyone inside in a powerful band of protection and energy, forcing the woman that Adramelech has just grasped hold of out of his hands and pushes her gently away, before looping around the demon, just in time for Marie Laveau to step into the circle.

Chapter 20

Power reverberates and curls around all of us. Snapping like a whip, it reaches out and circles around the demon king, forcing him to show his true face. A gasp echoes as if from one voice, rippling through the surrounding crowd, as bright red glowing eyes beam eerily out of a masculine face with admittedly amazing bone structure. Curving horns in a stunning golden red curve upward from his skull.

Adramelech looks a strange mixture of sexiness and evil, wrapped in a deliciously muscular body. A tempting package, if it weren't for his eyes. Thankfully, they happen to be a right turn off if ever I've seen one. Unlike his horns, which is just plain bizarre if you think about it logically.

I'm brought back from my wondering mind in time to watch Marie strut closer to the demon, until she stops a mere foot in front of him with her right hand on her hip, in what looks like a provocative stance.

"Is she trying to distract him or hit on him?" T.T. mutters to me out of the corner of her mouth.

"I have no idea. I'm hoping like crazy this is some weird ploy to distract him, but going by the way she's standing, I think we might need to come up with a plan B. Fast," I whisper in reply.

"Adramelech, you've been a bad boy. Don't you know you're not allowed in this realm no more?" Marie

Laveau practically purrs her question at him. A slight smile eases across her face. It's her hand twisting in circles behind her back which catches my attention more than anything else.

"What's she doing?" I mutter in confusion, out of the side of my mouth.

"Grave magick—don't forget she's a necromancer. Or was, at least," Felicity whispers back to me before carrying on chanting.

Taking the hint, I keep on chanting too, weaving into my magick an extra spell to prevent any unwanted backlashes, just in case someone decides to try and double-cross us.

"Protect us from harm
Remove this demon from our realm.
Protect us from harm
Return him to hell.
Protect us from harm
Right all wrong caused by his release.
Protect us from harm
Keep all safe and sound.
Protect us from harm
Return Adramelech to whence he came.
Protect us from harm
Let no harm befall.
Protect us from harm
On the departure of those that do not belong.
Protect us from harm
Protect us all."

Our chanting rises to a crescendo. The earth shakes beneath our feet almost tipping us on our asses. Thunder grumbles above our heads, and darkness descends for just a moment before turning an angry purple-black with orange spreading through it. Standing as steadily as we can, we push more power into our words, as the wind picks up and screams around us.

"You don't belong here, demon. Don't you feel the power of these witches surrounding you? They will send you back, and once more I'll help them!" Marie shouts into the gale-force winds, only to receive a mocking laugh in reply.

"You don't scare me. I am a king amongst you. Bow down and grovel at my feet, and I may just spare your paltry lives!" Adramelech growls in a pompous voice, while pointing an imperious finger at the ground in front of him. I don't know how I refrain from bursting out laughing.

Thinking about it logically, it probably has something to do with the fact that he's scary as hell when he looks directly at you. Which he's doing right now, making my poor insides want to curl up inside of me and cower.

This feeling feels alien to me and gives me pause to wonder why I'm feeling it. Breaking from the others around me, I move forward as I gather both my magicks to me, wrapping them around me as if they are a full shield.

"Be gone, demon; your tricks won't work on me," I calmly inform him as I build up a ball of healing light, pouring hope and love into it, before trickling it out and sending it to everyone around me.

I hear gasps of surprise coming from all around the clearing. And out of the corner of my eye, I see some of those surrounding me shaking their heads, as if coming out of a deep fog. I can totally understand, as I'd felt as if I was being held underwater and sound was muffled by my fear.

"I said bow down to me," the demon shouts as a flicker of uncertainty flashes lightning fast across his face.

"She don't listen to you; no one does anymore," Marie Laveau informs him. "Your time has long gone, and now it's time for you to go and never come back."

Standing beside Marie, I look at her and watch a look of satisfaction blaze a trail across her face as she brings her twisting hands forward, and I finally realize she's been twisting grave dirt in her hands. Bringing her hands up to her mouth, she blows the dirt into Adramelech's face and begins chanting, *Demon be gone; your welcome has reached its end*," repeatedly.

All of us join in her chant, our powers linking and combining, wrapping around the dirt and expanding it in golden chains of bright healing light, binding him in its power. His face and body distort, becoming monstrous in both size and appearance until finally, with a scream of pure unadulterated rage, Adramelech combusts into a twisting mass of black smoke before being sucked into the ground.

We keep on chanting until Marie indicates we can stop. I notice the spot where the demon had stood is now sealed over by a pentagram in a circle, with symbols entwined around and through it.

Looking closer, I realize that the symbols represent the different magicks used to seal away Adramelech. The moon representing the werewolves. A tombstone to represent the necromancers. A smaller pentagram in a circle to represent the witches. A blood drop, which I'm assuming represents the vampires. A part-human and part-animal head representing the shapeshifters. A triangle with a lightning bolt over a line inside it and a small circle beneath the bottom of the triangle is surrounded by a larger circle represents the voodoo community.

Feeling puzzled, I gaze at a twin lightning bolt, which I don't understand, before glancing at the final one, a triangle in a circle with a rose in its center encased in a web design. Looking at the triangle, I believe that it represents me, mainly because the rose and web design reminds me of my brands, which then makes me wonder if the twin lightning bolts is for Janna.

"It's time for me to go," Marie informs me as she peers down at the pentagram. "A word to the wise, be careful and watch your back. There is more between heaven and earth than the demon just departed." Without another word, she disappears, leaving me feeling more confused than before.

With a final look at the ground, I turn around and walk back toward the car with the others and then head into town for something to eat and drink. Personally, I'm starving and feeling this side of dehydrated. If I don't get something to drink soon, I'll be ready to be mummified. The true Voodoo Prince and his people decide to join us. Everyone is quiet, almost as if we're all wondering if that is the last of Adramelech we'll see.

I feel drained and uncertain and can't help but wonder, what exactly did Marie mean by her final comment?

Chapter 21

An hour later, everything feels much better with the world. Surprising what some food and drink can do to my outlook on life. I'm still no further along in figuring out what is going on. At least, though, we know we still need to go back to Paradise Falls, fingers crossed that some answers will come up between now and our arrival.

"Okay, I know it wasn't exactly easy *per se*, but did anyone else think that getting rid of one of hell's kings was just a little too easy?" Jasmine asks, while staring into her mug of coffee, as if the answers she's looking for might be revealed within its depths.

"What do you mean? Do you think it was some kind of test?" I ask, staring thoughtfully at my friend while remembering everything that happened.

"Yes. No. I don't know. It's just..." Shaking her head, she finally looks up and meets my eyes with her own puzzled look. "Honestly, I have no idea. It's just that with everything we've gone through already, I would have expected more of a fight from Adramelech than what he gave us."

"Same here," Selene agrees from across the table.

"Could maybe he have been surprised at us all working together or even been weakened by his previous incarceration?" I ask in a very hopeful tone of voice, even as my stomach sinks farther down, heading toward my shoes.

"Maybe…like I said, I just wonder if it's all over with him."

"Okay, how about we look over our shoulders until we know for sure everything is finished where he's concerned. Well, in our lifetime at least. The ground was sealed over with magick where he was standing, so unless that's broken, it should contain him. Should being the operative word, though." I mutter the final bit, feeling completely uncertain about everything that had happened in the bayou.

After all, it only takes one person to have worked against us in trapping the demon to make everything unravel slowly. A tiny chink in a spell can have dire consequences. Ones that might not be noticeable until it's too late.

"Look. Could the reason that it was so much easier than you all imagined be simply because there was so many different types of supernaturals working together?" suggests Victor, looking at each of us in turn with a slightly perplexed look on his face. "After all, that seal on the ground not only looked strong; it had everyone's magick on it. How often does something like that happen?"

I look at the other girls around the table and feel my lips twitch in humor. Trust a vampire to point out the obvious and in such a confused manner to boot. Bless him, he is seriously adorable at times.

"If I'm wrong—"

Shaking her head, T.T. interrupts Victor before he can say more. "You're not wrong. You just reminded us all of something we managed to miss." Letting out a little laugh of amusement, she continues on, "We're so used to dealing with just witch and necromancer magick, that we didn't even contemplate the effects of using all our magick, including vampire, voodoo, and shapeshifter. Those differences cause a humongous power boost, one we just never thought of."

"I must admit," the young Voodoo Prince adds, "if it wasn't for the fact that I was there to witness and partake in the magick, I would never have believed it to be possible." Shaking his head, he looks around at everyone. "I'm still not, though I know and felt it happen."

"I get that," Cedrix drawls as he watches the young man and his people through half-closed eyes, as if opening them fully would be too much effort. I'd believe it, if I hadn't caught the sharp gaze carefully accessing everyone. "Not every day such intense magick is used. Is it?"

I'm guessing by the quirk of his eyebrow and slightly puzzled expression, his question is a genuine one. I give a slight snort of agreement. "Hell, no, it's not normal to use that kind of magick every day. For that matter, it's not normal practice to use intense magick like that at all. Too dangerous," I add, to clarify my reason.

"Could you imagine having access to that kind of magick all the time?" purrs a young voodoo woman, as she practically drools at the thought of so much power.

I look sharply at her and the others in her group. Each looks thoughtful and…hungry. Casting a quick glance around, I notice those in my group looking at the others warily. A whisper of wind moves around and through us.

"Beware of bonds created by need, for they are

easily broken when greed takes over. It's time for you all to leave. Now!" Hecate's voice is barely a whisper, but her words ring loud and clear through me. I notice the others in my group looking nervously around them, as if wondering where the voice had come from. Well, all except Jasmine, that is. She quickly rises and grabs her stuff, and with an inclination of her head, says her goodbyes and heads to the counter to pay for her lunch.

Her sudden movement causes a ripple effect, as we all stand and gather our belongings. "It was nice to meet you all. Hopefully, we won't need to work together in such a capacity again," I inform the Voodoo Prince and his followers. Seeing his startled expression at our sudden departure, I quickly explain that we must go, before collecting my coat and following the others to the counter to pay.

Once we've all paid, we head outside and down the street. I drink in the sights, sounds, and smells of New Orleans awakening fully to the new day. Before long we arrive back at our vehicles, pile into them, and head off toward the airport. We need to schedule our departure on Janna's plane and head back to Ireland. It's time to return to Paradise Falls.

Chapter 22

An hour later, we've finally climbed on board. Janna has finished doing her preflight checks, and we've been granted clearance to leave. I'm feeling a slight buzz of anticipation ripple through me and half wonder what exactly Hecate meant by her warning.

"So tell me," Victor whispers into my ear, causing shivers of longing to tickle through me. "Did you enjoy your brief stay in New Orleans?"

Our faces are so close that our noses bump against each other's, when I turn my head to face him. Looking into his beautiful silvery-green eyes, I can't help the twist of longing that tightens the muscles in my stomach. "Yes," I reply on barely a whisper.

His eyes dilate as he stares into my eyes. I notice his throat moving as if he's just gulped. A slight smile curls my mouth upward. I love the effect I have on him, because he causes me to have the same reaction. Fair is fair after all. And, boy, do I want this man. My body is practically vibrating with my need for him, and a small ache is quivering low in my stomach, sensually delving down into liquid heat between my legs.

His nostrils flare as he breathes in my scent. His fangs descend as blue fire bleeds over his silvery-green eyes, swirling together as his emotions rise. I watch as if in slow motion as his right hand rises and the back of his fingers trace across the side of my face, brushing my cheekbone down to the corner of my mouth before lowering to circle my chin and raise my face to meet his eager mouth.

Our mouths are almost touching when he quietly informs me, "I want you more each second than the moment before. You're like a drug to me, highly addictive, sensually brightening the world around me, turning my life inside out, and I'm loving every second of it. Like an addict, I never want this feeling to stop, and I'll never give you up." The last he growls at me, before slanting his mouth across mine and plundering my mouth with his tongue.

Two minutes later, the floor vibrates beneath my feet, and we're taxiing down the runway, speeding up, and taking off. Funny how the actions of the plane mimic the emotions flowing through me.

Chapter 23

I read for most of the flight, though my mind keeps going back to that kiss and Victor's words, causing a smile to flit across my mouth and my hand to brush against it every now and again. About halfway through the flight, I give Victor more of my blood to drink in the bathroom.

We don't make out, even though I badly want to, and going by his groping hands, he does too. Still, doing it in a bathroom that's not mine is not on my fun list, especially in the only bathroom on a plane flying quite a bit above the earth. I don't think the others would be sympathetic to our desires, not that I could blame them if it was the other way around.

Feeling sleepy, I recline my seat backward and buckle myself in. Victor does likewise and pulls me toward him. I rest my head on his chest, and he lowers his chin down to the top of my head. Slowly, I drift off to sleep in his warm embrace to the gentle motion of his chest rising and falling.

Sometime later, I'm nudged awake by Jasmine, who informs me we're getting ready to land, so we need to raise our seats back up. I kiss my vampire lover awake, and together we return our seats to their proper position. Glancing out the window, I see the lush green grass of Ireland displayed before me. The plane swoops sideways, turning gently to position itself to line up with the runway.

"Why are we going to Dublin airport? I thought you lived in Cork?" puzzles Roísín, from her seat across the aisle.

"We do, but we flew out of Dublin airport and left our cars here. So now we need to collect them and drive back to Cork," I reply, feeling relieved to have gotten in a nap.

"Oh. You need to learn to fly, like my mum and dad so that you don't leave your car in the wrong airport in future," Roísín replies in such a matter-of-fact way that I can't help smiling at her. Kids. Everything's so straightforward with them.

"I do believe you're right," I reply, "but first I must get lessons and then a license before I can."

Nodding her head in understanding, she looks at me and beams a huge smile. "Yes, you must, then you can come visit me when I return home with my parents."

I can't help the smile that spreads across my face and the agreement that flows out of my mouth before I even think about what I'm agreeing to. What can I say? She's cute, and she lets me know when food's about, so how on earth can I resist her request?

Forty-five minutes later, we've exited the airport. Well, all of us except for Janna, Vincent, and Roísín who are flying to Cork airport where Victor and I will pick them up.

The journey back to Cork takes longer than expected due to ice turning the roads treacherous. A car speeds past us—granted, that's not hard as we're traveling at sixty kilometers an hour—but as it passes us, it hits a patch of black ice, swerves, narrowly missing the car in front, and slows down. Other than that, the drive is thankfully uneventful. Four and a half hours later, we arrive at Cork airport, and I'm busting for the toilet.

Victor parks the car in front of the entrance so I can jump out before carrying on into the short-term parking bay. I barely manage to dash around people instead of bowling them over as I make a mad dash to the loos. Finally, I arrive and barge into a vacating cubicle.

"Sorry," I call out to the woman who wasn't exiting fast enough.

"No problem. We've all been desperate at some stage," chuckles the woman in reply. Three minutes later, I exit the cubicle feeling like a new woman. Quickly, I wash and dry my hands, before I head toward the front entrance to meet up with Victor. I quickly phone Janna. After finding out where they are, I tell her to stay put, and we'll meet them there.

A few minutes later, Victor walks through the door. My heart picks up speed, and a smile blooms across my face. I dash into his arms as if I haven't seen him in ages instead of the ten minutes we've been parted.

"I've missed you," he murmurs into my neck before kissing me sweetly, his arms wrapped securely around my waist holding me to him.

"Same as. Feels like we've been parted for ages, which is just weird if you think about it." I chuckle in reply, before reluctantly extracting myself from his embrace. "Come on; let's grab some coffee before heading back home." Linking hands, we walk to the coffee bar where Janna and the rest are waiting. We quickly order a coffee and sandwich each. Once everyone has had their fill, we gather our belongings and leave. Ten minutes later, we're on the road once more.

Chapter 24

When we finally arrive back at mine, I'm surprised to see everyone hanging out outside, since it is bitterly cold out. Climbing out of the car once it's stopped, I spy Dante talking to Selene and guess the others are all unabashedly listening in. To prove I'm right, I go over and join them. After all, I can't find out what's going on unless I listen too.

"Selene, where you go, I shall go. You have my heart. I'm giving you my body too." Clasping her hand tightly in his, he leans down and kisses her knuckles while keeping eye contact with her the whole time. "You are my fated mate, my destiny, the other half of my heart, and I am yours."

I watch a blush stain her cheeks and can't help the grin that spreads across my face. Even though his words sound almost ridiculous in this day and age and rather lascivious too, the sincerity in his voice, eyes, and expression clearly tells Selene and everyone else that he honestly believes what he's saying.

The thing is, I believe him too. I believe that for some reason our soul mates are finding us. I have no idea why now, and granted, not everyone seems to be ready to admit it, mainly Cedrix and Jezebel. Though over the last week or two, they have become much closer, almost as if they're opening to the possibility of romance, if not love.

Which is fair enough. Only recently could I admit to Victor and myself that I love him. I'm not sure how far into their relationship Jasmine and Kheda are either, or if they even are in a relationship yet. All I know is that they've shared a room sometimes. Hmm, I must have a chat with her soon and get all the details.

"How about we all go inside where it's warm?" I ask, looking around at everyone.

I catch sight of Cedrix and Kheda. Both men are intently watching the women in their lives. I wonder if Cedrix realizes just how intently he's staring at Jezebel, almost as if she's his salvation and he doesn't know how to handle it.

While Kheda watches Jasmine like she's his whole world and he's just realized he's ready to take a leap of faith. Personally, I hope he does, as they both deserve the happiness they'll find with each other.

The crunch of gravel under a foot is my only warning before I'm embraced from behind.

"Love seems to be in the air." The deep growling rumble of his voice reverberates along my spine and tingles in my ear, causing heat to pool between my legs and a sigh of contentment to ease from my mouth.

"The things your voice does to me." It's only when I hear and feel his chuckle that I realize I spoke out loud.

"Don't worry, my beauty, you do wonderful things to me just by being you too" is Victor's husky reply as he slowly walks backward, his arm still around my waist so I'm slowly being dragged with him. Not that I mind, far from it in fact.

"I need to be inside you badly. I ache with the need." Nipping my neck gently, he takes another step backward, as I let out a low groan of need.

"Are you okay, Candi?" Roísín asks coming up beside me and looking at me with genuine worry.

"I'm fine, thanks," I squeak in reply, before clearing my throat. All eyes suddenly turn toward Victor and I. My friends give me smirks of amusement and some outright snicker at my predicament. I can feel heat stain my cheeks. Not from embarrassment over Victor's and my obvious need for each other. But because the heat crawling up me is desperate for release.

I need him now, and if he threw me on the ground and took me right here in front of everyone, I wouldn't give a shit. Well, as long as Roísín got safely inside and couldn't see.

"Are you sure? Your face is all flushed and Victor's supporting you…" Confusion laces Roísín's voice, and uncertainty flickers across her face.

"I'm fine, sweetie, honestly. Victor's going to take me to his house for a little while. I'm just feeling… fatigued. I need to lie down for a while."

The next instant, I'm swept off my feet and am curled against his strong chest. "I'll take you right away," Victor promises me. His eyes, I notice, when he looks at me are pure sparkling vampiric blue fire, and his innocent-sounding words spoken through distended fangs are a promise of pleasure soon to be had. I can't wait.

Between one blink and the next, he flits us to his house. Holding me to him with one arm, he runs his fingers down his door, and it swings open, allowing us entry into his domain. By the time the door has swung closed behind us, I've landed on his bed with him leaning over me, his mouth descending to mine.

****

"Brother, I don't understand. Are you saying you regret the path you have taken? Have you finally come to your senses?"

Staring out of my sister's apartment window, I look without seeing the streets of Paris. People scurry about their business as if my life crumbling around my ears means nothing. Just a blip on the screen, if even that. "I don't know," I finally admit.

"Are you being serious? How can you not know? You either regret the path you're on, or you don't!" Sophie exclaims in annoyance.

Turning around to face her, I shake my head in resignation before admitting, "I only regret hurting her by killing her parents. I don't care about the other deaths. I only care about…"

"Her." Sophie finishes my sentence softly. Moving closer to me, she looks at me with such deep concern I feel a shudder rake through me. "You worry me. This obsession you have with her, it's not healthy. But…"

Grasping her by the shoulders, I give her a slight shake before growling out in frustration, "But what? Say what you're thinking."

"Okay, if you know nothing can happen between you two, then if this obsession you have with her stops you killing more innocents, then you have to help her. You must leave The Protectors *once and for all."*

****

Our mouths meet in a kiss filled with passion and desire. My hands reach for his jacket, push it off his shoulders and down his arms before tossing it aside. I'm about to reach for the hem of his jumper when he brushes my hands aside to swiftly remove my jacket, jumper, and jeans. A groan breaks free from him as he stares in desire at my breasts cupped lovingly in my purple bra.

Bending down, he gives each pale mound an open-mouthed kiss, before lifting them out of their cups and suckling on first one nipple and then the other. My head falls backward, and my hands delve into his thick hair holding him in place. A moan of desire escapes me. I can't help it; it won't be contained.

With a final kiss to each breast, he moves lower down my body, placing fleeting open-mouthed kisses and licks across my torso until finally he reaches the top of my panties. These ones have the words "saucy" written across the front and "minx" across the back of them.

"Saucy, indeed," chuckles Victor on reading the front before peeling them off me. "Damn, you're so wet, I can't wait to slide into you." He groans before placing his mouth at my entrance and licking his way inside me. My panties are tossed in the direction of the rest of my clothes, then both his hands push my legs up and spread wider apart, giving him better access to me.

A shudder ripples through me as his talented tongue delves inside me. My hands grasp the bedsheets, before grasping once more a hold of his head and shoving him closer to me. His lips clamp around my nub, sucking it inside his mouth.

My back arches off the bed as my eyelids flutter. "Oh, oh yes," I cry out, as my chest heaves and the beginnings of my orgasm builds.

His right hand leaves my knee to slide up my leg. He inserts one of his thick fingers inside of me, curling it up and thrusting it slowly in and out. When he withdraws, he adds another and repeats the motions, hitting my g-spot with his talented fingers with each thrust. His tongue, lips, and teeth are tormenting me as they suck, lick, and nibble my hooded lady, licking me from front to back before clamping around me once more.

"I can't. I can't…"

"You can't what, baby?" he mumbles from his place between my legs, not even raising his head to ask his question.

"Hold on." I gasp as my walls clamp around his fingers, squeezing them.

"Let go, sweetheart; I got you."

I'm feeling too much, too quickly. My control has left the room and probably the building too. Thrashing beneath him, I try to wriggle away until he places his left hand flat on my torso, holding me effortlessly down as his fingers and mouth speed up.

My orgasm shoots through me, a scream rips from my throat, my back arches from the bed, and my toes curl up as my body shakes and spasms with the intensity of my release. I flop back, feeling like a limp noodle, and yet my body craves him deep inside me.

He places a final kiss between my legs before withdrawing from his position. I watch him as he slowly removes his clothes. Each tantalizing glimpse of his muscular body makes my heart rate pick up again and my mouth water in anticipation. I want him badly. No, I need him. I need him by my side no matter what. I need him deep inside me so I don't know where I end and he begins. I need him as much as I need oxygen. Maybe even more so.

Wow, I've gone from not being able to admit my feelings straight in the opposite direction. How can I possibly need him so much?

"What are you thinking about?" His hands have paused on the buckle of his belt. His beautiful torso is completely bare of clothing, showing me the ridges and valleys of his six-pack and impressive arms and pecs.

"God, I love your body!" I blurt out as my gaze travels over his beautiful torso.

"Thank you, but that wasn't what you were thinking of. Tell me!" It's obvious by his tone of voice and the shifting of his hands from his belt to his hips that it's not a question but a demand.

"Are you really not going to finish undressing?" I demand in surprise. Feeling slightly vulnerable in my nakedness both physical and emotional, I manage to pull myself up into a sitting position, draw my knees up to my chest and wrap my arms around them. Hiding my body as much as possible.

"No, don't ever hide from me, Candi. Be it thoughts or your body, never feel you need to hide from me."

I watch him as he moves around the bed, all power and grace and pure predator. When he reaches me, he sits down beside me, carefully taking hold of my hands and removing them from their protective grip on my legs.

Slowly, he removes my defenses, baring my body to his view. With each careful movement of his, my internal wall crumbles just a little more, until finally my legs are once more lying flat against the bed, slightly parted so he can see everything, and my heart is hanging wide open, bleeding my emotions all over the place.

"I need you," I gasp out, the words feel as if they've been ripped from me. "I need you completely, not just your body, but you. Your heart and mind. Your love and thoughts, everything." Once the words start spilling from me, I can't seem to rein them in. I feel as if a water dam has broken, and my words are spewing from it. "I can't get enough of you; you're like oxygen. Bloody vital to my every breath!" The last bit I shout at him, all control has escaped from me.

I launch myself down the bed to escape not just his watchful eyes but my words and myself. A strong hand grasps my ankle just as I've reached the end of the bed. *Damn Vampire reflexes!* "Let go," I growl in warning, feeling like I'll rip his head off in my need to run away.

"Never."

Chapter 25

Such a simple word. Such an immense impact. My body freezes. My arms curl around the bottom of the bed, where a moment ago they were trying to give me leverage to scramble away. One leg raised to kick backward to help in my escape, while my other leg is trapped by one flipping strong hand. Yet one word is all it takes to stop my flight. One. Bloody. Word!

"I'll never let you go," he informs me as he drags me back toward him. "You are mine, and I am yours. End of discussion."

"There was a discussion in there somewhere?"

Flipping me over as easily as if I'm a pancake in a pan, he gives me one more yank so my butt is at the edge of the bed, and his large body is wedged between my legs. Leaning forward, he grasps hold of my chin, keeping my face still, and maintains eye contact with me.

"No discussion, just a simple fact. You keep trying to run from your feelings, and I'm not letting you anymore," he growls the words out, practically spitting them in my face. "So you need me, and you're afraid of the fact. Fair enough. Now let me tell you something little girl. I need you too."

"Little girl?" I manage to sputter out before being harshly interrupted.

"Yes. You are mine. Your body, mind, and your

fucking soul is mine. Get used to it, sweetheart, because I'm never letting you go." Next thing I know his mouth has slammed down on mine. His kiss is one of punishment and domination. There's no gentleness in it at all.

Strangely enough, it's exactly what I need. I need to feel and hear that he's on this emotional roller-coaster with me. I know he loves me. He's far from afraid of telling me, *unlike me*, but seeing this fury and dominance coming from him is spelling out loud and clear what he's feeling, and it's like I suddenly know everything is going to be okay.

My hands descend to his buckle; quickly, I undo it and fumble with his jeans button and then slide down his zip. His penis is thrusting against my hand through his clothes, as desperate to come out and play as I am for him. Pushing his jeans and boxers down, I release his manhood, and it springs forward eagerly.

My hand eagerly grasps hold of him, and I lead him down to my entrance. Raising my hips, I wrap my legs around his narrow waist. So close I feel his head brush against my entrance. His hands leave my chin and ankle to unwrap my legs from around his waist, before knocking my hand away from his throbbing manhood.

Flipping me over onto my front, he yanks up my hips so I'm kneeling in front of him. Pushing one firm hand down between my shoulders, he keeps me in the position he wants before curling his hand around my hair.

Shivers of desire race through my body, and I wiggle my ass closer to him.

"Never, ever let your fears of our relationship become between us again!"

His words are growled close to my ear.

His thrusts are forceful, and when he twists his hips, I can't help the moan of desire that escapes me.

The hand that is wrapped in my hair gently but firmly pulls me up, while his other hand circles my waist diving down my body until his fingers reach my nub, where they start rubbing it. He nibbles along my jawline, before whispering in my ear, "Damn, girl, I'll never get enough of you."

I reach up behind me and grasp a hold of his head. My fingers dive into his hair and grip it, and turning my head, I fuse my lips with his. Our tongues dance with each other's, mimicking our bodies' thrusts and withdrawals. My other hand clasps Victor's, removing his talented fingers from between my legs and bringing them up to my breasts.

A moan of satisfaction leaves his mouth as he slams more forcefully into me. I let my hand slide down my body past my nub and reach a little farther back.

Soon, our rhythm speeds up, becoming more primal and forceful. I pant into his mouth gasping and moaning as my eyelids flutter. My body begins to convulse. I shatter and scream my release into his mouth, as my orgasm crashes over me.

A split second later, Victor's penis swells even more before he empties his release inside me. Ripping his mouth from mine, he roars his satisfaction before baring my neck and sinking his fangs into it, drinking his fill as his hips slow their thrusting to a more languid pace.

"Ohhh yes" is the only coherent thing I manage to gasp as my legs tremble uncontrollably.

Withdrawing his fangs from me, he pulls me

tighter to him and growls, "Never again forget you're mine, sweetheart. You have a worry, tell me. You're horny, come to me. Trust me, baby, I'll sort you out. No matter what, we're in this together."

Sinking back into him, a sigh escapes me, and all I can do is nod my head.

"I need your promise, Candi." His voice is a harsh whisper in my ear, yet it's his need that calls out to me.

It's hearing it that makes me realize that I've hurt him. I didn't mean to. Fear and uncertainty is something I'm not used to feeling. Scrap that, I'm not used to feeling anything like I do around and about him. A sigh shudders through me.

"Agreed," I whisper back. "But Victor, this goes both ways. If I'm yours, then you're mine, and you have to come to me when you have any problems, uncertainties, or needs."

"Oh, I can promise you, darling, I will come to you and only you." Slowly, he pulls out of me, gently lowers me to the bed. Pulling back the blankets, he picks me up as if I weigh nothing and positions me in the middle of the bed before joining me. He pulls the covers over us and then wraps his arms around me, kisses me on the forehead, and whispers soothingly to me. Finally, I nod off, content and at peace.

I'm not sure where my uncertainty had come from. All I know is that Victor's fierce handling and controlling tone has put my fears firmly in their place. Breaking them into little pieces and crumbling them to dust.

I also know if they resurface again, this time I will talk to him, instead of trying to run away. I feel my eyes drift closed and my body become lethargic. Wrapped in the safety of Victor's warm embrace, I drift off to sleep.

"Are you sure we should be doing this?" Vivian asks me in a hushed whisper, looking nervously around the street and back to the alley before us.

"Should be? Probably not. Have to? Sadly, yes. The last time Victor and I were in Whitechapel, this alley appeared, and we'd also read about it too," I reply in just as quiet a voice, while glancing around to make sure no one was watching us. "Somewhere inside, the Shadow World holds answers that we need."

"Yes, but what are the questions?" T.T. demands in an aggravated tone of voice. She never was one for riddles.

"No idea," I admit, which gains me frustrated looks and loud exhales of exasperation from the others.

"Look." Victor interrupts the grumbles that have started up. "We all know this situation isn't ideal. And yes, I do know that is the understatement of the year," he adds before anyone can even open their mouths. "What you have to remember, though, is this is new to all of us. So don't go putting added pressure on Candi or ask for certainties you know she can't give."

I look at him and smile, my heart filling with happiness, simply because he defended me. Reaching toward him, I link my hand with his and give it a squeeze. He's right. Come what may, we are in this together.

"All right, bitches, cut your whining. Let's get this over with," Jezebel instructs while carefully moving forward and closer to the alley entrance.

"Don't forget, no matter what, stick together, and mind where you walk. You don't want to be swallowed by a dark spirit," I add, making everyone freeze.

"Whoops, did I forget to mention that part?" I ask, feeling exceptionally guilty. After all, it is a rather important factor.

"Yes" is the unequivocal answer.

"A what?" mutters Cedrix, looking mightily confused and slightly worried.

"Stick with me. We'll keep each other out of trouble," Jezebel replies as she moves back toward him to take his hand.

As one we enter the alley and straight into the Shadow World.

Chapter 26

Bolting upright, I gasp in a breath while looking through sleep-encrusted eyes around me.

"You're safe, sweetheart. You're at my place in Paradise Falls," Victor reassures me while rubbing circles on my back in gentle motions.

"I just dreamt we were all in Whitechapel."

"Tell me what happened."

"We were standing at the mouth of the alley. We were all there, except for Roísín and Janna. They were at your house in Whitechapel. We were discussing why we had to go through. You stood up for me." Turning my head toward him, I lean closer and place a chaste kiss on his lips.

"No one wanted to go through, but we knew we had to find the answers that are there. As we don't know the questions…"

"Ah, I see, the unknown questions can be seriously frustrating."

"Exactly. Then I remembered to warn them about the dark spirits." I notice Victor wince and guess he's remembering our last encounter with one. Though he hadn't seen it, he had heard its furious scream when we'd managed to escape from it. "Yes, as you can imagine that didn't go well, though…"

"Though what?"

I smile at the puzzled expression on his face and

with a slight laugh tell him about Jezebel and Cedrix.

"They're opening up to each other. I noticed in New Orleans that they'd become closer and more at ease with one another" is his only reply. Well, that and the gleam in his eyes.

What is he thinking about in that busy brain of his?
"Do you think we should—?"

"No."

"But I haven't even finished what I was going to say?" I huff, feeling slightly baffled at his apparent knowledge of what I'm thinking.

"No matchmaking. Look, they'll get together at their own pace. Think of it this way; we're still finding our footing, and we don't have the whole jumping-bail-and-chasing-after-her situation."

"You're right."

"I am?" Victor asks, sounding completely wary of my sudden agreement.

"Yes, you are. We just had a killer trying to kill us is all, so you're right. What is a little hunting and running compared to that?"

"Very true," Victor agrees, before calmly carrying on, "At least, though we knew about magick and didn't find out about it by having the woman you're following turn into a jaguar or anything and then her friends do magick in front of you and explain your parents were killed because they were a different species, and guess what, you're not actually human."

"Ugh, that is so not fair. You can't throw that into it. Okay, I know it must have been a shock for Cedrix, but surely he's over it by now?"

"It only happened a couple of weeks ago!"

"Okay, okay. Fine, you win. No matchmaking. So,

Dante and Selene…"

"Oh my God, you actually can't help yourself, can you?"

I stare in surprise as my sexy lover bursts out laughing, and for a second I wonder why. Shaking my head, I begin to laugh too. "I never was a matchmaker before," I finally admit.

"You're seeing soul mates come together, and you're trying to hurry them up. Sweetheart, you have to let them go at their own pace, or…"

"Or what?"

"Or they might let fear of the unknown drive them away from their partner, unless said partner refuses to let them go."

"Oh."

"Sound familiar?"

"Just a little." Putting my right hand up, I put my thumb and index finger close together to show the little gap between them. "We're talking about us now, aren't we?"

"Yes. Just a little bit."

"Do you think that's what happened to me? Fear getting in my way?"

"Yes. I'd always hoped to find my soul mate. To find the one person I could love and who would love me back, no matter what." Taking my hands in his, he looks me straight in the eyes. "While I was ready, I don't believe you'd even thought about a long-term relationship, never mind finding your soul mate. Had you?"

Shaking my head, I extract my left hand from his to stroke his face. "No, I hadn't. Though I am so glad I found you," I admit, before leaning into him and kissing him.

The ringing of Victor's cell phone interrupts us, followed a split second later by the chiming of a text coming from mine.

Grabbing up my phone, I read the text message that came through. In shock, I reread it three or four times.

Candi, I'm back. We need to talk. Grandma Eve.

Chapter 27

I stare dumbfounded at my phone. As if by doing so, further information will come. Something along the lines of where the hell my grandmother disappeared to for starters. Or even why she did. Or, I don't know, what the hell she was thinking by practicing dark magick.

Any extra little bit of information would have been helpful. I get zilch. Nada. Sweet F.A. I'm not impressed. In fact, I'm feeling pissed off right now as I glare at my silent phone.

I get dragged from my internal fury by Victor informing whoever he's talking to on the phone that he'll tell me now. Turning to him, I raise an eyebrow in inquiry. Then swallow at his tight expression. Whatever he's about to tell me doesn't look like good news.

I sit on the edge of the bed and lean my elbows on my knees and my chin in my cupped hands and wait for his conversation to finish. *Please don't let the news be too bad* is all I can think. The words chase around my head repeatedly, becoming a mantra.

Finally, Victor says thanks and goodbye to the person on the phone. He hangs up and slowly turns to look at me. The look of uncertainty on his face is such an alien one I feel instantly floored. *What on earth could be so bad to cause such an expression?* Fear dances along my spine making me shiver.

"Just tell!" The words squeak out past my tight throat. Sitting straighter, I wrap my arms around my waist as if to protect myself from the unknown.

Victor slowly, almost carefully moves closer to me. Kneels in front of me, placing both his large warm hands on my knees, giving them a slight reassuring squeeze.

"Oh God, how bad is it?" I demand in surprise.

"It's about your grandmother…"

"What? She's back. I've literally just received a text from her, so…" My words trail off. I honestly can't figure out what is going on. "Has something happened to her? No." Shaking my head at my own query, I know that's not right as Victor was already on the phone when my grandmother texted me. "Tell me what exactly was your phone call about."

"It was Big Michael on the phone. The demon finally talked. Well, he'd tried to get ahold of me when we were abroad. I was meant to return his phone call…" Shaking his head as if to clear it and reorganize his thoughts, he then carries on, "Candi, your grandmother and her coven of dark witches were the ones who called the demon to this realm. When the demon impersonated your grandmother, it was to steal your magick. She was to lead you…"

"To George Seabast the Fourth's house," I mutter, remembering the demon trying to dash down an unknown path leading back to George's house. Shaking my head in wonderment, I feel as if pieces of a jigsaw are beginning to slot into place.

"Yes. Which is why some of the lower members of *The Protectors* were there. Apparently, if the information gathered from the demon is correct, your grandmother and her coven were about to join them. They just needed to prove they were strong enough to do so first."

"I'm sorry, what? No." Shaking my head in denial, I honestly can't wrap my brain around this newest turn of events. "No, no way in hell was my grandmother joining *The Protectors*! They killed her daughter. My mother."

"I know." He grasps my hands that have started flying in the air with my words, holds them tightly to his chest, calming me as I feel his warmth and the steady thump of his heartbeat. "Candi, I think she changed her mind, which is why she left without a word. Except that warning she sent you through a text. I don't think she could go through with it after all."

Unshed tears blur my vision. I take a deep shuddering breath and stare into the warm gaze of the man I love. "She was going to sacrifice me to gain extra power. I saw the darkness surrounding her that last day. Now I know why."

Victor draws me to him, wrapping his arms around me. He rubs my back in soothing circles and kisses the top of my head. Tears trickle down my cheeks as sadness engulfs me. Followed swiftly by anger until I remember when Eve took me in after my mum died. How heartbroken she was.

She was devastated, just as I was. I left and joined the army to move on with my life. To begin a fresh chapter. Her life was here, no new start. Can I honestly blame her for going dark?

Pulling back from me just enough so we can make eye contact, Victor speaks to me in such a calm and soothing tone that I can't help listen to him. His words instantly stop my brain's ramblings.

"I know you're hurting, and believe me I understand that you feel betrayed. The thing is though, I think you need closure. Talk to your grandmother, though not alone and definitely somewhere public. Best not to take a chance."

"You're right."

"I am? I mean you agree?"

I can't help the slight laugh that escapes me at his puzzled tone and expression. "Yes, you are, and I agree. I do need to know, and I most definitely need to be sensible in meeting her." I feel my back straightening with every word I say. "She might have had a wake-up call and gone off to sort herself out, or for all I know, this could be another attempt at gaining more power.

"What hurts the most is that I honestly don't know if I'm about to walk into a setup. Before this conversation, I would never have thought my grandmother was even capable of willingly hurting someone. Let alone me." Wiping a hand across my face, I swipe away my spilled tears with a slight smile trembling on my lips, I lean forward and kiss the most beautiful vampire I have ever met.

"Come on, my beauty; let's get showered and dressed, then go meet up with the others. We can then discuss a plan of action for your grandmother and Whitechapel too." Rising to his feet, he gently pulls me to mine, before swooping me into his arms, carrying me off to get cleaned.

Chapter 28

Hugging my mug of coffee, I look around my sitting room where my friends are currently staring at me in shock.

"Are you serious?" Jasmine demands, with a slight quiver in her voice.

"Sadly, yes, I am," I reply with a nod of my head to confirm my statement.

"Your grandmother, though? Oh, Candi, I am sorry," Selene sympathizes. She's sitting on the floor next to Dante, her hand linked firmly with his. I have a feeling if he had it his way, they would always be linked together.

"So what do you want to do?" quizzes Jezebel, from where she's sitting on the floor between Cedrix's legs. I feel surprised that she chose to sit there, I know space wise there aren't a lot of places to sit with so many of us in the room, yet for her to choose to sit between his legs and lean against him…This is huge for her and maybe for Cedrix too.

"How do you want to handle it?" asks Janna, in the bluntest tone of voice I've ever heard her use. She's sitting on the sofa with Vincent in front of her and their daughter Roísín on his lap. They all look exhausted, as if the stress they've been under for so long, now that it's over, is finally catching up with them all.

"We've decided." Since Victor is sitting on the

floor between my legs, I place my hand on his shoulder, to indicate who "we" are. "It'd be wisest to meet somewhere public where all supernaturals can go. I think Hal's Diner is the best bet."

"Makes sense. It's close enough, yet away from witches' lands, and there's plenty of room for all of us to go but not make it obvious we're all together," Kheda agrees.

"I think Janna, Vincent, and Roísín shouldn't go," Victor informs everyone, while staring at the three in question.

"What? Why?" Vincent demands sounding slightly hurt at being excluded.

"Because with everything you've all been through already and with the trip to London and the upcoming fight, I think you should all spend time together and gather your strength while you can," Victor replies in such a practical no-nonsense tone of voice, it's obvious his reasons are purely for their best interests and no other.

I watch understanding and relief flicker across Vincent's face and wonder if he'd thought Victor didn't trust him or blamed him for his mother's actions, even though he'd reassured him that wasn't the case. Though it's not surprising that he has doubts. After all, centuries of blaming himself for his mother's actions wouldn't be easily put aside, even with reassurances.

"Okay, sounds like a plan of sorts. What we could do is go into the diner in groups. Say Cedrix, Jezebel, and Talia, you three could go in and find a booth toward the back.

"While Selene, Nancy, Vivian, and Dante, you can go in together and find a booth at the front. Leaving

Kheda, Jasmine, and Felicity to find a booth near the middle, close enough to Victor and I, to hear without being too obvious." Looking around at everyone, I see nods of agreements. "If everyone's happy with that, I'll make the call and phone my grandmother. Once I know she's meeting me, we'll head off in separate cars. Each table group per car to make it easier and five minutes' gap between each group leaving too. Agreed?"

"Agreed," everyone replies.

Fishing my phone out of my pocket, I dial my grandmother's number. Once she's answered the phone, I get straight to the point.

"Can you meet me in twenty minutes at Hal's Diner to talk?" I ask her.

"A hello would have been nice, Candi," she scolds me in such a perturbed tone I feel like laughing.

"Really? Well, a good-bye and an explanation would have been nice too, so we're both disappointed, aren't we?" Silence greets my answer, and after a few minutes, I check my phone to make sure she's still on the line. Finally, she lets out a large sigh.

"I suppose I deserved that. Can't you come over to mine so we can talk privately?"

"No. I need to get something to eat, and Victor will be with me, so Hal's Diner or nowhere."

"Victor? Who is Victor?" Confusion laces her voice, and it's only then I remember she never did meet him.

"Victor is the man I'm in love with…"

"Really? Well, bring him…"

"He's also a vampire, hence neutral ground."

"I'm sorry, what?"

"Will you, or will you not meet me in Hal's

Diner?" I hear my gran inhale loudly before exhaling in a whoosh. Talk about letting me know she's annoyed without saying anything.

"Fine. But do you really have to bring a vampire with you?" Disdain drips from her voice straight into my ear over the word vampire. As if the mere mention leaves a bad taste in her mouth.

"Yes, I do," is my only reply. I honestly don't know how I refrain from lashing out at her or changing my mind altogether about meeting her. All I can think of is the fact that she set a bloody demon after me, yet she's being nasty about my dating a vampire. Concern isn't even in the equation here.

Victor turns slightly so that he can look at me and rubs his right hand in soothing circles on my leg. Taking a deep breath, I look at him and give a nod and a trembling smile to let him know I'm okay now.

"I'll see you there in twenty minutes," is all I say before hanging up. A shudder passes through me, and I suddenly feel exhausted.

"Hey, it'll be okay," Victor informs me, turning around so that I'm now cradling his hips between my legs as he kneels between them and leans into me. "We're in this together, no matter what. Okay?"

I look away for a split second trying to gather my thoughts, but he grasps my chin firmly between his fingers, forcing me to look at him. "Okay?" he repeats looking me intently in the eyes, searching my expression for my answer.

"Yes," I finally say. "We're in this together, no matter what. But if you want to back—"

"No. Not happening. No-matter-what doesn't have an escape clause, sweetheart, hence the whole, no-matter-what part." His tone is teasing, and his beautiful full lips turn up at the corners; yet his eyes, well, they're far from teasing. They are serious and determined, and filled with promises he'll keep.

Looking into his gorgeous eyes, I can't help the feeling of relief that washes through me. Reaching out, I trace the angles of his face, lean forward, and kiss him.

"Thank you," is all I manage to say once I pull back slightly. Taking a second, I look at the others in the room. "Okay, guys, you ready for this?"

"Nope, far from it, so let's get this over with," Jasmine answers, causing everyone to go still before bursting out laughing.

"Fair enough." I chuckle, turning a teasing smile on my friend just in time for her to give me a wink. "Okay, let's get this show on the road." One by one, everyone gets up and heads off to the cars and then the diner. I turn to Janna before I leave. "This house has a warning system in case anyone comes onto the land who means harm. If anything happens…"

"We won't take any chances. Now stop worrying about us. We'll be fine; you need to worry about yourself. After all, it's your heart on the line here."

Biting my lip, I give Roísín a quick hug before turning toward the door and leaving. There's nothing left to be said, so waiting around won't do any good at all. Deep in my heart, I know that Roísín, Janna, and Vincent are better off here than with us. No way in hell do I want any attention being brought on them, and especially Roísín. After all, it's not every day a Daphmire and her daughter stroll into town.

Chapter 29

Sitting across from my grandmother after all this time seems weird, to say the least. Especially with my vampire lover beside me and my friends spread around the diner for added protection.

The idea of needing protection from the woman who loved me and took me in after my parents were murdered, seems so bizarre I'm waiting for the punchline in a joke to happen. Sadly, this situation is so far from being funny, I'd probably end up knocking someone's teeth out if it turned out to be a hoax.

"I don't know where to begin," I finally admit.

"How about with why he's here?" my grandmother asks, pointing a finger in the direction of Victor while refusing to look at him.

"Actually, no. How about we begin with why a demon was impersonating you, then claimed that you had sent it after me?" I oh-so-calmly inquire.

I watch as my grandmother stiffens, tension flows through her, almost pulsing. She opens and closes her mouth a couple of times before swallowing. She reaches for a glass of water and swallows a large gulp. Her hand trembles ever so slightly. I would have missed it, except for the fact that I'm watching her so closely.

"When…" Her voice croaks. Taking a calming breath she tries again. "When did you find out?"

"Ah, so you're not denying it. I had wondered if

you would. Hoped that it wasn't true."

"It's true."

I stare in shock at the woman who taught me about magick. Who I loved before I met her. I remember the stories my mum used to tell me about Grandma Eve, and how much she loved her. Staring at the woman before me, I wonder for the umpteenth time, what the hell happened to her?

"What the hell happened to you?" My words fire out of my mouth like a machine gun going off. Hitting their target, going by my grandmother's flinch. I don't care. I just want and need answers now. "Tell me." My words are ground out between my clenched teeth; my jaw aching from the grinding of my teeth.

"Does it matter?" Shaking her head at her own question, she lets out a sigh. "Stupid question. Of course it matters," she mutters. Looking up, she finally looks toward Victor and then back to me again. "I've been in denial for a long time. After your mother's murder, I couldn't handle the sadness I was feeling. Teaching you about magick helped, yet the speed at which you took to it wasn't natural.

"It was as if you'd been born practicing magick. You excelled at it and soon were doing spells that most witches couldn't do. Hadn't been able to do in centuries. I became jealous. Then you left and joined the army."

I stare at her in shock. Everything I remember now has a different slant on it. More sinister. Where I'd assumed she was hurting from the loss of her daughter, it now seemed it was jealousy over my magickal abilities.

"I became angry and unreasonable," Eve continues,

apparently unaware of the turmoil rolling inside of me due to her words. "Soon, I was talking more and more to other witches who were dissatisfied with their abilities. We began practicing together and harnessing magick from other sources."

At this point, Victor takes my hand and squeezes it, letting me know I'm not alone, as I stare in growing horror at the woman before me. A woman I'd always thought of as gentle and caring, not...power mad.

"First, it was only sifting magick from weaker witches, or duds who had a trace of magick that was lying dormant inside them. Useless to them, but to us... Anyway, it wasn't long before we made small sacrifices, a bird or rodent. Eventually though, that wasn't enough, so we moved onto cats and dogs, then larger animals."

Taking a deep breath, she looks at me once more before her eyes slide downward. Tracing a water drop down the length of her glass, she finally admits in a very quiet voice, "Eventually we made a human sacrifice. Oh, the power we harnessed was phenomenal." A groan of satisfaction escapes from her, as her eyes slide shut, as if remembering brings on the euphoria she apparently felt.

A shudder of revulsion sweeps a path through me. I feel physically sick at what I'm learning. Glancing at Victor, I notice that he's looking grim.

"We knew that if we could gather so much power from a mere human, the power we could take from a supernatural would be spectacular. Then you came back to town."

"What?"

"It was like you offered yourself. Just when we

realized we needed more power, you came back, and we could feel you. You'd somehow managed to grow even stronger than before. Being near you was like a drug.

"Sally and Savannah, they came up with a plan for draining you, though I believe that had more to do with wanting him—" Nodding toward Victor, she scowls at him as if this is his fault. "—than with your powers." Eve sends Victor a baffled look, as if she still can't understand why anyone would want him, before continuing her story.

"I devised the plan of calling forth a demon to remove your magick; I knew you would be too strong otherwise. It was Evelyn, though, who wanted us to join *The Protectors*. All those supernaturals at our mercy— we would have free range to cull the herd, so to speak. Drain the power we needed while…"

"Murdering people like your daughter?" Victor probes in a calm conversational way, even though I sense the deep-seated rage rolling off him in waves.

"Like my daughter and granddaughter. It was only when the plan came into action that I realized just how far I'd fallen. I couldn't…" Closing her eyes, she takes in a shuddering breath before opening them to look directly into mine. Her gaze pleads with mine for, I don't know what, maybe understanding. But I don't understand, and I don't think I ever will.

"I didn't know what to do. I'd gone so deep down the path, I wasn't sure if I could climb back out again. So, I left."

"Why didn't you warn me?" I demand. "You sent a fucking demon after me and then had a change of mind, but nooooo, a simple warning was too much?" I practically scream at her. My voice is a hoarse whisper-shout, as I don't want to cause undue attention, yet at the same time, my need to rail at her is overwhelming me.

"You're right. I should have. I'm sorry. I'm so sorry." Tears slide down her pale cheeks, and her lower lip trembles.

I look at her and realize I really don't know her at all. Shaking my head, I say the only thing I can think of. "Why did you come back?"

She pauses midswiping of her eyes to stare in confusion at me. "Because this is my home. Candi, this is where I belong. I only went away to get my head straight and detox from the magick…"

"Hold on. You went away for a couple of months to a magickal rehabilitation center?"

"Yes…"

"And it only took a couple of months to detox years' worth of addiction?"

"Well, no, not exactly…"

"What exactly then?"

"Now, Candi, you must understand—"

"No, Eve, I don't have to understand at all. What I know is that you went off the rails, had an epiphany if you like, and went to detox for a very short while, and now you, what, think everything should be all grand and hunky-dory now that you've seen your way straight?" Shaking my head, all I can do is stare at her. "Honestly, I don't know what to say," I finally admit. I feel exhausted. Completely drained.

"I came back because I needed to warn you. *The Protectors*, they're gathering together. They're preparing for war."

"I know."

"No, you don't. Candi, they're building an army of supernaturals and humans…"

"I know."

"Don't be stupid, girl. There's no way in hell you can know! There's more going on here than even I knew about!"

"Do not call her stupid, old woman," Victor growls in such a threatening way, I half expect him to rip my grandmother's head off.

I run my spare hand gently down his arm, petting him and calming him down.

"Old woman," splutters Eve in shock. "How dare you?"

"How dare he? How dare you, I think you mean," I answer in such a ferocious whisper my grandmother sits farther back into her seat as if to make sure there's plenty of distance.

"Me?"

"Yes, you. You, who stole and killed for magick that wasn't yours. Who might as well have spat on my mother's, your daughter's, grave, due to your actions. Who was going to join *The Protectors*, for fuck's sake! And finally, who set a demon after me, your own grandchild. And why? Simply because of greed." Shaking my head, I look at her before standing and tugging Victor after me.

"Wait, where are you going?"

"Away. Away from you, and other than that, it honestly doesn't concern you anymore." I turn to walk away but pause after only a couple of steps. I glance back at the woman in the booth and admit to her, "You broke my heart. You ripped up my memories and showed them as falsehoods. I thought you loved me, only to find out you loved and coveted my magick."

Swallowing, I blink away the tears gathering in my eyes and look once more at her. "Goodbye, Eve Allhallows. Lose my phone number; you're no longer part of my life."

"Candi, wait. Please. I know you're angry, but you can't be serious. We're all we have left…"

"No, see that's where you're wrong. I have family, and they're right here." I see a look of relief wash over her expression. A feeling of guilt assails me as I hadn't been thinking of her. Stomping on it, I explain, "My family is here." I point to Jasmine's table. "There." I point to Jezebel's table. "And there." This time I point to Selene's table. "And right here." This time I place my spare hand on Victor's shoulder. "I also have some family waiting back at my house too. Where I don't is in that booth you're sitting in." I know my words are horrible, even saying them causes pain inside my chest, yet it doesn't prevent them feeling true.

Without a final word or look, I turn on my heel and walk out the diner with Victor beside me and the others standing and following me outside. In silence, we head to our cars, climb in, and drive back to mine. The drive home is silent except for the odd hiccupping sob coming from me as unchecked tears slide down my face.

Chapter 30

Once we arrive back at mine, we sit in my car for a while. At some stage, Victor must have unbuckled my seatbelt and dragged me onto his lap. I only know this because I'm curled up on it as I soak his t-shirt with my tears.

"I was so mean to her," is all I can wail out, before convulsing into louder tears.

"Shhh, you weren't. You had a shock is all, a rather large one, granted."

"I did, didn't I?" Sitting back slightly, I wipe my tears away with my hands. "I just don't know what to do," I finally admit, while staring out the window.

"How about we go inside? Maybe get something to eat and just take a time out, hmmm?"

I give a nod of agreement. A time out sounds good to be honest.

In silence, we climb out of the car and walk to my front door. Jasmine opens it before we reach it, steps outside, and gives me a fierce hug. "You okay, hon?" she whispers into my ear while petting my back.

"Yes," I reply, to which I receive a snort of disagreement. "Okay. No, I'm not." I admit on a shaky laugh. "I'm so confused. I wish I knew if there was something I could have done to stop my gran before she went so…"

"Bad?" Pulling back slightly so she can look me in

the eyes, Jasmine gives me a slight shake. "Now, you listen to me, Candi Reynolds. I'm only going to say this once. This situation with your grandmother is not your fault. There was nothing you could do to prevent it.

"In fact, it sounds to me like your leaving probably saved your life. Your grandmother's actions are hers and hers alone."

I open my mouth to say something. I'm not sure what though. I don't get a chance as Jasmine carries on lecturing me.

"I know you're hurting right now from what you said to her. What you should realize is the simple fact it's now up to your gran to fight to stay in your life. She should make amends. Completely. We have a battle to prepare for, and I need, we all need, your head in the game right now. I'm sorry."

She gives me another rib-cracking hug before releasing me and walking back inside. Taking a moment to collect my thoughts, I give a nod of my head, look at Victor, and with a trembling smile reach out and take his hand. I give it a squeeze before releasing it and move forward to enter my home with Victor on my heels.

I come to a startled halt in my sitting room doorway, only to get knocked through by Victor walking into my back. Fast as lightning, he grabs me by the waist preventing me from doing a face plant on the floor.

"You okay?" His voice rumbles above me. Suddenly, his hands loosen, and I'm guessing he's noticed our guest. Before he drops me, he tightens his grip and pulls me to my feet.

"Nina, what are you doing here?" I ask feeling

confused as hell.

"Apart from watching you fall over yourself, you mean? I came to ask if you would visit the hospital. There've been more deaths, and I need to know what the hell is going on there!"

"Your sister, is she still there?" I inquire, hoping like crazy that nothing has happened to her.

"Yes. She's…weaker though. I don't like it." Fear and desperation flicker across her face before she locks her emotions away, turning her expression blank.

"Okay, we'll need to get something to eat, and then we'll head over to the hospital," I inform her.

"Eat? Are you kidding me?" she shouts furiously at me. "I just told you my sister…"

"We need to eat to make sure we're capable of facing whatever is there," I calmly inform the distraught woman.

"You know what it's like, Nina. Keeping energy levels up is too important and can make all the difference. Add into the situation that we have no idea what's going on…" I trail off. A shiver slithers down my spine as I remember standing outside Jasmine's hospital room waiting for her to dress so we could sign her and Kheda out.

There had been something very wrong about the smell of the hospital, making us all feel uneasy, and that was before I'd seen what I'd at first thought to be a doctor or nurse checking in on the patients. Well, right up until I realized the being I was looking at had no face. At all. Thinking about the faceless being I'd seen in the hospital corridor, I can't help wondering again, *had it been Death?*

Chapter 31

We've just finished eating when I have an idea. I'm unsure if it'll work and hesitate to mention it, yet my brain keeps coming back to it. After five minutes of internal debate, I look up to find everyone looking curiously at me.

"So, have you decided if you're going to share your idea with us or not?" Jezebel asks from where she's leaning against the wall with her arms crossed over her chest.

"How did you…?"

"Your thoughts are incredibly loud, also you had a debate flickering across your face," Selene answers, sounding and looking highly amused.

"So tell us what you thought of," Nancy demands, giving me a no-nonsense look.

"Okay, I'm not sure if it'll work though…"

"Just tell us. If it's a crap idea, we'll let you know, don't worry," T.T. cheerfully informs me with a smirk.

Shaking my head at her, I take a moment to collect my thoughts into some kind of order. "So, I had this thought—well, first I was wondering if it was Death I'd seen that time in the hospital…"

"What?" exclaims Janna in shock, staring at me with a wide-eyed expression. I notice Vincent looking just as baffled and Roísín looking slightly scared.

"Did you guys not know…oh, okay." I try to

reorganize my thoughts again. "Right, so I saw a faceless person who disappeared in the hospital. We think it might be Death."

"Oh, dear God. Your way of informing people of information needs to be worked on," Janna mutters, as she rubs the bridge of her nose.

I notice the others give slight shrugs of their shoulders and wonder what they're thinking for just a second before my brain gets back on track.

"Anyway, I was thinking that maybe we should do a spell of sorts before going to the hospital."

"What do you mean by a spell of sorts? Surely something either is a spell or isn't one?" enquires Victor looking as puzzled as he sounds.

"Normally, yes. What I'm thinking of, though, I'm not even sure it'll work."

"So why did you bring it up?" demands Nina in obvious frustration, while glaring at me as if she would love to wring my neck.

"Because the idea won't leave me alone. Which gives me the impression that it'll work."

"What do you need us to do?" Felicity inquires, while staring calmly at everyone, almost as if daring anyone to question me further.

"I need everyone outside and in a circle. I'll go upstairs and gather what I need." Decision made, I get up and leave the room. Ascending the stairs, I hear everyone start moving about. I hurry to gather the items I need, refusing to listen to see if anyone says anything. Though to be honest, apart from shuffling feet, I don't hear a sound.

Once I've got everything, I head downstairs and outside where I find everyone has gathered into a large circle leaving a space for me to join them between Victor and Felicity.

Breathing deeply, I center myself and enter the circle. Moving to the middle, I place a map of Paradise Falls on the ground and two candles on the edges to hold it in place. Then I add my bowl of salt to the middle of the map and splay my deck of Midnight Mystic Oracle cards facedown around them all.

Stepping backward, I move into my spot in the circle, where I notice everyone staring in confusion at my strange layout.

"Join hands, everyone, and whatever you do, don't let go." Once we've all joined together, I close my eyes, thinking only of what I want to accomplish.

"In this circle of might and power,
I form a ring of protection around us,
Bringing forth the power of Earth."

On these words, the salt in my bowl rises and spins, as if on a gentle wind and drifts around the circle, landing on the ground behind us, enclosing us in its protection.

"Let the spirit of Fire burn bright as the sun,
Cleansing the hurt and harm from all."

The candles ignite, the flames jumping higher than should be possible.

"As Earth and Fire join us this day,
Let the cleansing feel of Water wash away all fear."

A light rain trickles above the circle landing only in the bowl the salt had previously occupied.

"With the elements of Earth, Fire, and Water,
Let the spirit of Air join to protect all within this circle."

The wind picks up, bringing forth a leaf to dance in the circle, as a gentle breeze drifts around us all.

"With the spirits of all the elements here,
Let us see what must be seen.
In the heart of the Falls of Paradise,
Where sickness lies, and hurts befall,
An entity stalks the weary. Show us what it is.
Help us in our quest, to stop the faceless one."

My voice shouts out the final words, and power rumbles from me. The map pulls through the bowl until it's raised into the air, yet not a rip is visible.

My cards are gently buffeted by the wind until four rise from the ground. One above, one below, and one to each side of the map.

The bottom card shows a Blood-Moon, the card of change. Normally, epic wars and pain follow a Blood-Moon.

The card on the right shows a Graveyard, the card of death. But the card on the left pictures a Silver Fox, the card of deceit. These two cards together make me gasp in surprise. Slowly, I look up, to the top card, the card that will seal the others into place. The Golden Chalice. I feel relief wash through me at seeing this card.

With a nod of my head, I close the circle, thank the elements, and all return to their places as if they'd never been used or moved.

"I don't understand. What just happened and what did those cards mean?" Nina demands, while looking nervously at all of us and the items in the middle of the circle.

"It means," I say as I walk into the circle to gather up my belongings, "that it's not Death stalking the corridors. It means that there's a trickster involved who's draining the patients of their powers. And that war has been stirring for a while, unbeknown to us, yet it's not too late."

"Wait, you said the person was faceless," states a confused sounding Nina.

"Yep, because I saw no face."

"And it disappeared. You said afterward they disappeared. How can it not be Death if it was a faceless person who disappeared?"

Turning to her, I look her in the eye. "I don't know, but we will find out. This is magick of the cruelest type. Magick done against those already weakened and in a defenseless state of mind."

I feel my heart sink into my shoes when I realize I need to talk to my grandmother. See if she knows anyone practicing dark magick who would stalk the hospitals. *Ah hell, how exactly am I to ask that kind of question?*

"Shit, black magick," mutters Nina, oblivious to my internal debate.

"I'm going to make a phone call and see if a likely suspect can be thought of who might be doing this," I mutter to Victor before heading inside to return everything to my room and phone my gran in privacy.

Ten minutes later, Victor finds me staring at my ceiling, clutching the phone tightly in my palm.

"Candi, are you okay, sweetheart?" His voice soothes my frayed nerves, and I finally feel like I can breathe again.

"Yep, never better," I reply, before groaning in frustration. "Did you know that *The Protectors* are connected to one another?" I ask, guessing that he wouldn't.

"Connected, how exactly?"

"They link with one another, apparently. So that they can find each other and siphon power to who needs it from each other. Rather creepy, if you ask me."

"They're all connected to each other?" Rubbing his temples, my poor lover looks as if he has one hell of a migraine coming on.

"Yup. Actually, no, not quite. What my gran said was each section is connected to each other."

"I don't get it."

"Neither did I. It's like an army; hah, that's funny as that's exactly what they are." I snort, wondering if I've jumped on the crazy train without knowing it.

"Okay, like different levels of the army, how?"

"The first level is the recruits. The second level is the soldiers. The third level is the sergeants, until you get to the top, where you have the ones in complete control. Now, each level is connected by a blood spell."

"So what happens when you progress from one level to the next?" Frowning at me, I can tell he's trying to grasp the extent of what I'm saying, just like I'm trying to figure it out.

"What I gathered from what I was told is to safeguard each level, they unlink the blood spell and reconnect it with the next level."

"What the fuck? The amount of magick involved to do that would…"

"Need constant replenishing. Which with every kill and draining one member does, the rest siphon from them. I think this is why the hospital is in such a dire state. Someone is concentrating on the one spot to collect magick."

"Bloody hell!" exclaims Victor, while staring at me in shock. "Did your grandmother have any idea who would do this?"

"No, we'll have to go to the hospital and see if we can either find the person or at least a trace of them to hunt them down."

"Candi…" My name is all he manages to say. Watching his expression, I'm guessing he's trying to figure out how to say or ask what's on his mind without hurting me.

"Just say or ask what you're thinking."

"You're right. How did your grandmother know this? Is she one of them? Is she blood-linked and officially one of *The Protectors*?"

Shaking my head in the negative, I once more stare up at the ceiling. I feel his strong fingers grasp my chin, bringing it gently to align so we're on eye contact level. "Sweetheart, talk to me," he quietly implores me.

Reaching out, I stroke his face. Such a simple action, yet the contact helps ground me to the here and now. "The night she was 'kidnapped' was her initiation night. I was to be hers and the others' ticket in. They would have siphoned me, and the members of the lower level would have made the blood ties."

"Ahh hell, I'm so sorry, love." Releasing my chin, he wraps his arms around me, dragging me to him before kissing the top of my head. "On the positive note, they didn't manage it. Your grandmother saw the errors of her ways, and you knocked a demon unconscious."

I can't help it. I burst out laughing at his words. The tension in me eases, and I nod my head against his chest. "Yes, on the positive side, that is very true," I agree. My words are mumbled yet hold just a tiny hint of amusement in them. *Goddess, I really love this man.*

"I know you do, and he loves you too," Hecate whispers to me.

Chapter 32

Once more, it's agreed that Roísín and Janna stay behind. This time though, Vincent comes with us. We gather together outside of the hospital and move into our separate groups. Victor, Nina, and I will enter the hospital to visit her sister. This way, there will be two witches entering and two staying outside, as well as one officer entering the building and a detective outside. Covering our bases, so to speak.

Upon entering the hospital, we're assailed by the smell of death, porous wounds, and disinfectant. I want to vomit from the stench.

"Bloody hell, it's worse than last time," mutters Victor, his nose pinched and his lips barely parting to speak. I almost feel like laughing, except that would make me open my mouth, which no way in hell I'm doing.

"I told you it's gotten worse," croaks out Nina through clenched jaws. I notice her eyes watering, and wonder if it's the smell or the helplessness of her sister's situation. Probably both.

I indicate with my hand for her to lead the way. If I can keep from talking, then all the better.

We climb the stairs and head straight to Nina's sister's room. A little girl of maybe ten is lying in the bed, her tiny body barely making a bump in the bedding. The sight breaks my heart while the stench makes me want to retch.

Pausing in the doorway, I glance around. Seeing nothing, I open my senses and allow my magicks to merge. Shadows flicker into view, latching onto the little girl in the room. Sending out tendrils of magick, I let it flow around the room, sealing the windows and doors until finally I light it up.

The room turns blindingly bright violet and yellow. Screeches erupt from the shadows, and they try to flee through the exits only to bounce back and become entangled in my net.

"Holy shit," gasps Nina. I ignore her and concentrate on my trap, a net of magick, spelled to lock in on its captive, unable to feed any power from it.

I call it the Goddess Trap. So much power unattainable to mere mortals, unbreakable, yet though it detains, it won't harm. A magickal dampener. No magick can be used inside it or against it from the outside.

We hear a noise from down the hallway. Victor moves toward the doorway to look. The trap allows him to pass as it only captures those who mean harm. With the shadow's essence captured, the rest of the traps we set will seek out its signature and should help us find the person siphoning the magick.

Turning to Nina's sister, I look at her again and notice the shadows have all gone from her. I blast her with healing light, lighting her up. Her back bows off the bed, her mouth opens in a silent scream, and health rejuvenates her.

"Take your sister and take her outside, then send in Felicity to me. Tell her to keep the Goddess Trap active. She'll know what I mean."

I bind the sisters in protective magick, allowing them to leave and not be harmed by anything until they reach the others. Then with a look at Victor, the two of us slip from the room to find the maker of the noise we heard. Somewhere in this hospital, a member of *The Protectors* lurks, and they know we're here. They would have felt us breaking their shadows over the little girl in the bed.

Chapter 33

I leave Goddess Traps in every room we search. The patients we find will have to be healed later. At least now, their magick and life energy won't be siphoned anymore.

Silently, we move through the corridors. Floor by floor, we search until finally only the basement is left. I look at Victor and can't help wondering two things.

"Where are all the staff?" Victor mutters. I can't help smiling as that was one of the things I'd been wondering. The other simply was why the fucking basement? In every horror movie I've watched, bad things happen in the basement. Guaranteed.

Taking the stairs, we carefully descend until we reach our destination. The sign for the morgue greets us. I can't help the groan that escapes me when I remember the last time we were here and met Santa's lookalike. A shudder runs down my back at the thought of the twinkly-eyed narcissistic man. Dr. Sam McKenzie.

"If a morgue in a basement isn't bad enough, throwing that doctor in is just pure mean," mutters my sexy vampire, with a fair amount of disgust in his voice.

I give a grunt of agreement before moving forward. We pass through the doors and hesitate. Sounds of life come to us. I can't help the nervous glance I give the morgue door, before Victor taps me on the shoulder and points farther down the hallway.

I almost laugh when I see the sign for Staff Canteen. Terrible place to have it, but as we hear sounds of movement and talking, I can't help the feeling of relief that washes through me.

"Okay, what are we doing here?" Felicity asks from directly behind me, causing me to jump and scream behind the hand that's slapped across my mouth.

My heart is pounding so loud and fast I'm surprised no one hears it. Removing Victor's hand from my face, I turn to glare at my friend.

"Sorry, I thought you'd heard me." She chuckles in glee. "Not often I get to startle her," she explains to the grinning vampire beside me.

Shaking my head, I catch her up on what we've done so far. Then throw a Goddess Trap into the morgue before we enter.

Entering the morgue, we find no signs of life, so we check out the bodies filling the fridges and the trollies. Every fridge is filled. There are more dead bodies than room, not a good sign at all. Almost all the corpses have dark gaps in their auras, where they've been sucked dry of their magick and life essence.

"It looks like the medical examiner isn't sure what the majority of these people died from, going by his notes," Felicity whispers to us as she reads the files in front of her.

"Sounds like it's nothing to do with the creepy doc," I mutter. "Okay, let's move on then, as there doesn't seem to be anything here."

Quietly, we slip outside and head farther into the bowels of the hospital. We search the rooms we pass, all except the cafeteria. No way in hell could we explain our presence there. Instead, we place a Goddess Trap outside the door and send it under the gap. Just because we can't enter doesn't mean we can't seal the room. Exiting the end of the corridor, we find what appears to be an unused staircase leading upward. Peeling paint and stacked chairs give us the impression it's not been used in years. Especially with the slight mildew smell wafting from the corners and the layers of dust covering the furniture.

It's the footprints that tell us differently. With a grimace, I look at my companions and nod to them. We all agree we should step only where the unknown person had.

Chapter 34

"Do you reckon we should get Kheda, so he can arrest whoever we find?" whispers Felicity in my ear. I almost groan at her words and give her a quick nod of agreement. Best play it safe and have an officer of the law with us.

"We could always just do a citizen's arrest. After all, surely Kheda would need a warrant to search up there?" Victor interrupts before Felicity can retreat back to the door.

We both pause and stare at him. Going by his chuckle and what I can see of my friend's wide-eyed owlish look, we're doing a fabulous impression of two blinking owls.

"Excellent point, so who wants to go first?" I ask.

"You should. You're the one with the crazy badass powers," my fellow witch and friend encourages.

"Gee, thanks, sweetums," I sarcastically reply, while rolling my eyes and moving forward. A large hand lands on my shoulder, stopping me from advancing farther.

"I'll go first."

Looking up into his gorgeous silvery-green eyes, I see concern and love for me shining brightly. I give the hand on my shoulder a reassuring squeeze, lean up, and kiss him.

"She's right, I should go first." I pat him on the

chest, knowing by his growl that he's not happy for me to be first. "But you should go second," I add, causing his eyebrows to rise in inquiry.

"You want me to watch that fine ass of yours, no problem. Now explain why you can't watch mine, while I go first!" his voice rumbles low and throaty.

His beautiful full lips are flattened as far as they can go, his eyes narrowed while vampiric blue fire bleeds into them, and his skin stretches taut over his high cheekbones. His hands grasp my arms in a firm unrelenting grip, almost as if he wants to shake me or lift me up and place me behind him. Maybe both.

"Because I have the Goddess Traps and two types of magick to help me. I'll be using both to make sure there isn't anything up there that isn't visible to the naked eye."

A growl of dissatisfaction vibrates through his body. His sharp nod tells me he knows I'm right, yet it's his fierce yank dragging me to his hard body as his mouth slams down and devours mine that lets me know he's not happy about it.

"Damn," Felicity murmurs, sounding slightly in awe of his protective alpha ways. "Hey, handsome, you have to release her. You'll be right behind her to protect her, but we gotta get this show on the road."

With a final tonsil-teasing swirl of his tongue, he releases my mouth and steps backward. Giving a grunt of discontent, he peels his hands from my arms and glares at me as if by doing so it'll change the fact that I'm going first.

As quietly as possible, the three of us ascend the staircase, being careful to step only in the footprints already visible. I look through my double magick vision. My wolf peering out of my eyes overlaid with my witch's magick turns everything violet tinged and brighter than normal. Shadows become visible, and things wanting to be hidden show brightest of all. Like the footprints leading into the wall, which had been covered by a film of magick to hide them. Sending out two Goddess Traps, one up the staircase and one toward the wall where the masked footprints lead, I pause to see what happens.

A split second later, the wall beside us trembles before crumbling into pieces. Inside the hidden room is a witch I'd seriously hoped I'd never lay eyes on again.

"Ah fuck," mutters Victor from directly behind me, "maybe it's best that Kheda isn't here."

Chapter 35

"How did you find me?" demands Sarah Sullivan, anger rippling from her, pulsing in the room.

Ignoring her question, I ask one of my own. "How the hell are you here? I thought your ass got arrested?"

"I was let go the same day." A sneer curls her mouth as she looks me up and down. "All I had to do was cry how my evil sister was all to blame. How I had no choice. Idiots believed me."

It doesn't take me long to realize this girl has jumped on the crazy train with no intensions of ever getting off. She's also filthy and stinks to high heaven.

"How long have you been here?"

"Since the moment they released me. I knew your friends were here, so I decided this was where I was going to be." She flashes me a look of such satisfaction I can't help feel wary. "All these meat bags and the constant supply of magick at my fingertips. Perfect for supplying the energy my sister needs as well as the others." She cackles, actually cackles, and sounds totally demented while doing it.

"Christ," mutters Felicity as she peers over Victor's and my shoulders to gape at the filthy woman in the room. "How exactly do you know her?"

"She tried to kill Jasmine and Kheda. She and her sister murdered God only knows how many people and liked to keep trophies," Victor informs her.

"What kind of trophies, or do I really not want to know?"

"You seriously don't want to know; it still makes me feel sick to think about," I mutter to her out of the corner of my mouth while weaving my Goddess Trap larger not only to encompass Sarah but also to connect with those siphoning her magick. Like a large fly swatter, it'll knock them all out and cut them off from the source.

I feel my magick click into place and with a prayer to the Goddess Hecate I release it. Violet, silver, and bright yellow power erupts from me, howling around the room like a screaming Banshee. It twists in a circle, swirling and crackling like a tornado with flashes of lightning erupting inside it.

Wrapping around the crazy witch, tendrils seep into her, delving through layers of magick and into *The Protectors* connected through her blood link. Pulling the stolen magick back through the link and dispersing it back to those it was stolen from.

The witch's screams shatter through the circling storm, sounding like thunder erupting and vibrating throughout the room, until finally the trap secures her, binding her in its power. She crumples to her side, sprawling in a contained frozen state, her mouth hanging open and her eyes wide, staring blankly into space.

"Holy shit on a brick! What the hell was that and is she okay?" demands Felicity pushing past Victor to gawp at Sarah.

"I think she'll be okay?" I can hear the question in my statement and feel my brain has a WTF bouncing around my head.

"Could it be because of the connection to the others?" Victor asks through what sounds like a slightly strangled voice.

"Probably," I mutter in reply while feeling completely dumbfounded. *Bloody hell, I hope she'll be okay.*

It's only when we see her eyes blink that we all release a breath.

"How about we bring her outside to Kheda and Nina so they can...do something with her?" asks Victor.

"Sounds good to me," I readily agree, while looking wearily at the magickally bound witch.

Victor gently brushes past me to enter the room. He wearily reaches down and picks her up, carrying her out of the room in a fireman's lift. We retreat down the stairs the way we came up. This time, though, Felicity leads the way with me covering our backs.

I can't help feeling torn between enjoying the view of my sexy lover's ass and the fact that he's potentially in danger of the demented witch hanging over his shoulder. I keep a tight rein on my spell making sure she stays confined but not harmed.

By the time we've exited the hospital, I'm ready to scream from stress. I do not like the man I love being near a woman who would happily drain him of his life energy to share amongst her freaky-ass minions.

"What the blooming hell is going on?" demands Nina when she notices the unconscious woman. "Is that...?"

"Sarah Sullivan, yes. She's also the one who's been draining and sharing the life essence and magick of the patients," I inform her before turning to face the hospital and call forth all the traps I'd placed.

A few minutes later, we hear startled sounds, and then numerous traps come flying from the building before us. Each contains dark shadows, though one also holds George Seabast the Fourth. He, like Sarah, is unconscious, though beginning to awaken.

"Oh, good God, this day just keeps getting weirder by the second," I mutter in disgust.

A moment later, I hear Nina talking to someone on the phone and realize she's calling the police station when she gives them her name and badge number, before requesting a van to collect Sarah and George.

Ten minutes later, the dark shadows have disappeared as the energy holding them releases back to the patients, severing the connection completely from all who were draining them, and a police van has arrived to take away Sarah and George.

Nina informs the officers that she'll come to the station after she's taken care of her sister. Turning to us, I'm surprised to see tears in her eyes as she thanks us for rescuing her sister and the other patients.

"You can go now; there's no need for you to come to the station," Nina informs us while stroking her sister's hair back from her face. "I'll write up a report about what happened here; though truth be told, I'm unsure how to explain those two," she adds turning to glance in the direction of the retreating van.

"You sure you don't need us to give a statement?" I ask, glancing down curiously at her.

"I'm positive. Detective McKnight, I'm guessing you'll be going with them. If you send a report to me, I'll file it. Thank you for helping me. After the way I've treated you...thank you."

"I'll send you the report," Kheda informs her, before indicating we should leave. Turning back to her he asks, "Do you need a lift somewhere, you and your sister?"

"If you don't mind, I'll accept. My parents live in the housing estate off Lagoon Road. If you could give us a lift, I'd appreciate it."

Everyone piles into the cars. While Kheda and Jasmine drop off Nina and her sister, the rest of us head back to mine. Once there, Talia, Felicity, and I take a drive to the local supermarket and buy some food for dinner.

The girls receive a couple of curious stares, probably because they're new in town, but as they're witches, we don't cause too much attention, though I do see some customers talking in furtive whispers and glancing in our direction.

Once back home, we make dinner and give our statements to Kheda, who goes and hands them in to Nina at the police station. We then make plans to fly out to London the next afternoon. In the morning, Jasmine and I need to sign the papers at my solicitors.

The deeds for Jasmine's house and the land I'd specified had been drawn up a couple of months ago, but with everything that had been going on, we hadn't a chance to sign them, something I want to rectify before we leave for London.

Victor also wants to check in on the builders tomorrow before leaving and see how his pub is coming along. Jasmine decides she'll meet them too and see if she can hire them to rebuild her house, once they've finished with the pub.

Decisions made, we discuss sleeping arrangements.

Kheda and Jasmine opt to sleep at Victor's house as Jasmine will be coming with me in the morning. Janna, Roísín, and Vincent, and Cedrix and Jezebel also come with us, leaving the others to sort themselves out. I wonder if Dante will be going back to his house or staying. Then I wonder where exactly does he live.

Deciding my brain hurts and I don't care that much right now, I instruct my handsome vampire to take me to bed. I receive a lascivious smile and a smack on my ass for my trouble. Thirty minutes later, I'm in his bed, and my eyes are drifting closed. I'm exhausted. Curling myself around his big body, I stroke his firm chest and slowly drift off to sleep.

Chapter 36

Once more, Victor and I fly to London. This time though, the others have come with us, and we fly in by private plane, courtesy once again of Janna. I could get used to it, much more comfortable and a darn sight easier, in my opinion anyway.

We hire cars and load up with our luggage and sleeping bags. We all agreed to bunk together at Victor's house. Granted, it'll be cramped, but none of us mind.

Upon arriving at Durward Street, I carefully look around before exiting the car. The last time Victor and I were here, we were almost attacked by a dark shadow, a vicious entity that I hope never to see again. As one, we quickly grab our stuff and hurry into the house. Vincent, Janna, and Roísín are given one of the bedrooms. Victor and I drop our stuff off in his room, leaving the others to decide who's having the third room and who's sleeping in the sitting room.

There's a flurry of movement, a couple of squeals of laughter, and scuffles as people are forcibly removed from the stairs until finally silence. No sound. No nothing.

I glance around and wonder if I'm still in the house. Seeing Victor raise his head and look at me with a puzzled expression, I gather two things. The first, I'm still here. The second, I'm not the only one startled by the lack of noise.

Together, we creep toward the bedroom door and peer out. Encountering an empty hallway, we hear faint noises, but other than that, everything is silent. We slowly descend the stairs. It's only when I notice slight movement to the right that I realize everyone's in the kitchen hunting through drawers. Nancy has the kettle on and enough mugs laid out for all of us.

"We need to get food and milk," Victor informs me, breaking the quiet. His words seem excessively loud and startle everyone out of their thoughts. Turning to the others, he informs them we'll be right back, takes my hand, and leads me outside.

I quickly glance about the street to make sure all is safe, and then in silence we walk to the local shop, just enjoying the normality of it. The simple fact of walking hand in hand. Buying food together. It gives me a warm fuzzy feeling inside as well as a hope for the future, something to look forward to once we come out the other side of the impending battle ahead of us.

Before too long, we're back at the house, eating sandwiches and guzzling coffee. The silence is eventually broken when Vincent asks the question playing hide and seek with my thoughts.

"How are we going to do this?"

Sighing, I drop the rest of my sandwich onto my plate and look up.

"I don't know," I admit, glancing at the others. I hesitate before continuing. "I think…I think we should try to enter the Shadow World. It's where I dreamt we went and also…"

"Also what?" Victor asks quietly, from where he's sitting beside me.

"I'm not sure." Looking up, I turn slightly so I can look him in the eye. "I have this feeling that we need to draw the battle lines there. Almost as if...it's the one place we might have a chance."

"Are you thinking that because the portal was opened and so many spirits were sent there by *The Protectors?*" demands Jezebel, while staring at me intently as if she'd like to root around my brain and inspect my thoughts. A rather disconcerting feeling, if ever I've had one.

"Yes." Nodding my head, I stare back at her before looking around the room. *Maybe they need to see what I saw to understand my logic?* It's only when I see everyone start in surprise I realize I'd said that out loud.

"You can do that?" Dante demands, looking slightly flustered at the thought. "What exactly are you?"

I can't help but laugh at his question. "Sorry," I apologize at his disgruntled look. "It's not the first time I've been asked that."

"Probably not the last either," chuckles Selena, turning to Dante she adds, "Poor Candi has been asked that by everyone in this room, and to answer your question, she is unique in more ways than one. She's the Double Magick one, from the Prophecies."

"You're not serious, are you?"

Instead of answering, I decide to figure out how to show everyone what I saw. "*Remember it, and they will see*," Hecate whispers to me.

Taking a deep breath, I close my eyes and picture the scene I'd seen in this very kitchen. A second later, startled gasps sound. Popping my eyes open, I'm once more greeted by men, women, and children being brutally removed from their homes by members of *The Protectors*. This time, however, we're shown what happened next, the rape and massacre and the opening of the portal. Of how, even in the Shadow World, these souls were persecuted, mainly by Rose, Vincent's mother.

"Gather allies from those amongst the persecuted. Together, the living and the dead will fight for freedom." Hecate moves silently into the room with her hounds at her side, startling everyone. I notice some of my friends paling in disbelief as they realize who stands before them. While others stare at her in confusion, knowing that before them is an entity of great power, yet not realizing who or what she is.

Kheda, Jasmine, Victor, and I stand, each of us cup our right hands in our left and place them over our hearts and bow to her.

She gives us a slight inclination of her head and continues, *"The battle ground has been chosen. It's time to bring the beginning of the end to fruition. Be careful, though, for none of you is safe until the Prophecy is complete."* She looks at each of us in turn, inclines her head at us before simply vanishing.

"Bloody hell," exclaims Cedrix, looking slightly shell-shocked. "Who exactly was that?"

"Hecate, Goddess of Witches, the Underworld, Crossroads, and Magick," I reply. "I did tell you the gods and goddesses were real," I add with a wink at his dumbfounded expression.

"I thought you were joking" is his muttered reply, before turning a wide-eyed gaze on the others. "Did you all know?"

"Umm, no, well, yes, but I didn't think…" babbles

Jezebel who looks seriously spooked.

"I can't believe that happened to those people," Roísín says to her mum, her lip trembles as she turns to look at me. "You saw this happen before?"

"Yes, sweetheart. Well, some of it and only for a split second."

"You have to stop them from doing it again. Promise me you'll stop them!"

I feel my throat tighten and swallow around the lump that has risen in it. All I manage is to strangle out two words, "I'll try."

I think she realizes that I can't promise anything. Hecate said it herself; there is no guarantee that any of us will survive this coming battle. And I refuse to make a promise unless I know I can keep it. Especially a promise to this little girl. A child that has already been a victim of *The Protectors'* minions.

Chapter 37

Night finally falls. One by one, we slip from Victor's house, all except for Janna and Roísín. No way in hell are we taking a child into a potential war zone. Dressed all in black, we creep across the darkened street to reach the alley.

Looking around at everyone, I remind them to watch out for dark spirits and to stick together no matter what. Grasping hold of Victor's hand, I give it a squeeze before stepping forward and into the Shadow World.

A thick mist covers the streets before us, making everything darker and more cloying than I ever imagined it being. Glancing at the others, I realize I can barely see them even though they're directly behind me. Even Victor whom I'm holding hands with is barely visible.

"Candi, maybe we should cast a link spell so we don't lose one another!" exclaims Talia, strange how even her voice sounds so far away.

"Hold on, don't do it yet," I call back to her, before quickly casting a ball of light which I hold in front of me. Finally, we can see each other, the shadows and mist retreating from my light. I notice something slithering away. I have no idea what it was and hope to never find out.

"Okay, everyone, gather around and hold hands."

"I'm not going to start singing some song," jokes Nancy, as she quickly grasps hold of Selene's and Vivian's hands.

I grin back at her, before releasing my ball of light into the middle of our circle and grabbing hold of Jasmine's hand with my now-empty one.

"Okay, let's magickally link together so, even when we drop hands, we'll be unable to lose one another." Glancing around the circle, I nod to my two fellow witches as one we start to chant.

"Bind us who are linked together,
Hand to hand so we shall stay together.
Even when separated in this world,
Join us together so we can find each other.
Link us now by thread of magick,
Link us together until we are ready.
Magick weaved on this night
Protect us from darkness
Protect us from all."

A delicate-looking violet and gold thread weaves between us, wrapping around our hands, linking us together, as if we're joined by skin and bone. Once the circle of linked thread is complete, it simply vibrates and disappears.

"Umm, guys, I can't see the thread anymore. Does that mean it didn't work?" Dante asks, while looking worriedly at Selene. *He looks terrified that she'll disappear before his eyes, bless him.*

"No, it worked. Everyone can let go now." I try and release my hands from the firm grips of my lover and friend. "Seriously, you can let go, it worked." I laugh, shaking my hands free from their firm grip.

A slight ping echoes around us, and a tiny beam of

light pops up over my head. "See that?" I ask my stunned-looking friends. "Each one of us will have one of them flashing above your heads. Once, that is, you let go of each other." I watch as they reluctantly release each other's hands, and then they all ping as a light pops up over their heads.

"And how exactly does this help us?" demands Jezebel looking crossly at her light.

"The best way is to show you. Hold on a sec." Quickly, I run down the street and hide in a doorway. I hear cursing coming from my group and recognize Victor's voice.

"Hey, it's okay. Look, there she is," Felicity quickly reassures him. The next instant, I'm grabbed and thrown over his shoulder and carted back to the group.

"Seriously, Victor, you can put me down. I was only showing you that we can't lose each other, no matter where we are," I exclaim as my head bounces against his firm ass. Receiving no answer, I decide to just bite him.

"What the—?" I suddenly find myself standing in front of him as he gives me an incredible look. "I can't believe you just bit my ass!"

"Can't blame her. That is one fine ass," T.T., mutters, not very quietly to Felicity.

"Don't do that again," Victor growls at me, as he shakes me slightly by the shoulders.

"Which, the biting you or the demonstration, 'cause I thought you liked me biting you," I tease him, which is apparently the wrong thing to do. Who knew?

Once more I find myself slung over his shoulder, his hand pressed firmly over my ass. "Seriously? Come off it. We can't do what's needed properly if I'm hanging like a sack of potatoes over your shoulder," I scold him.

"Victor, a word for just a second, please." Vincent grasps hold of his elbow, gives me an apologetic glance, and leads us away from the others. "Guys, you need to claim each other properly, or this crazy behavior will only get worse."

"Claim each other properly how?" Victor and I say at the same time, causing Vincent to swear, then rub his hand down his face.

"Seriously? Oh Christ, I'm not surprised the two of you are getting so emotional. You need to bite each other at the same time—"

"We've done that lots of times," interrupts Victor.

"Have you then claimed one another as your other half through the link?"

"Umm."

"I'll take that as a no, as if it wasn't obvious you hadn't already," mutters Vincent in exasperation. "Guys, fucking hell, how have you not either killed each other or someone else yet? Don't you know that claiming each other is more than an emotional connection; it's a matter of sanity. It's about admitting to one another you're soul mates. That you belong to each other and only each other.

"Claiming each other through the link bonds you together through this lifetime and allows you to sense where you are even if you're not together. It's a primal force, and bloody necessary for your own peace of mind."

"Does that mean he can safely put me down now?" I ask. "Seriously, the blood is going straight to my head. I'm feeling slightly woozy."

"Christ's sake, put her down!"

Safely once more on my feet, I lean against my overprotective partner as I'm feeling lightheaded; thankfully, his arm is wrapped around my waist holding me up.

"You can't do it while linked to everyone else, but the moment you're not, bite one another and through the link claim each other."

"Any particular words?"

"As long as you say 'I claim you as mine,' you'll be fine. Seriously, how did you not know this?" Shaking his head at us, he then escorts us back to the others. I feel like a naughty child coming back from the principal's office. Going by the look on my beloved's face, he does too.

"Y'all sorted out now?" drawls Cedrix, raising an eyebrow in enquiry.

"I'd be able to take you more seriously without your bobbing light," I tease him, to which I receive a smirk in return. "We'll be fine, once this is done and we've sorted something out," I add, while rubbing circles on Victor's back.

"Okay, so what now? How do we…" Nancy trails off what she was saying as we hear the distant sound of feet pounding along the pavement. Glancing at each other, we head off down the street after we affix our link to the alley. No point being able to find each other if we can't escape this world afterward.

Chapter 38

We hurry down the road, my light ball bobbing overhead illuminating our way. A scream of terror echoes through the night, shattering the silence, quickly followed by a laugh of joy and a taunt. "Here, ducky, ducky, come out and pllllaaayyyy. You'll know I'll catch you. And the longer you make me hunt, the worse it'll be," roars the voice of a laughing man.

The shadows grow thicker, more intense, almost as if trying to protect someone. A little farther away, I hear the faintest sound of a stifled sob. Glancing at the others, I receive a nod of confirmation that they'd heard it too.

Growing closer to where we'd heard the sound, I see a shadow come through the fog and a flash of a blade as if an arm is swinging it. "I know you're there, and soon you'll join the other specters of the night," chuckles the man.

A human form darts away from the thicker shadows, running in our direction, clinging as much as possible to the side of the houses, as if to take cover.

"I see you now, little ducky. There's no escape for you. My blade is dying to meet you," laughs the man in joy as he chases after what appears to be a woman.

"Oh, fuck this; I can't see shit," I mutter in disgust, not knowing if this is an elaborate game between two hunters hunting us, or if the figure coming at us quickly is truly a victim.

I stand still in the middle of the street, bend slightly forward toward my toes. I gather power to me, rolling it up my legs from the ground itself. Crackles of light flash. Green, silver, violet, and gold swirls of raw energy merge together, spitting bolts of lightning, only to be drawn back into my energy ball.

I hear the footsteps falter but pay no attention. With a feeling of raw anger washing through me, I throw the power I've gathered into the air, fling my arms wide open, and shout at my fullest volume.

"Shadows of the night and realm take form once more. War has brought you here, and war will set you free.

"Gather yourselves together, reclaim what you once were. Shadows of this land, it's time to fight back against *The Protectors*!"

The energy ball bursts apart, swirling and diving throughout the Shadow World. Streaks of lightning flash and spark, while thunder booms and ripples across the night sky gathering the mist and breaking it apart, until, finally, light fills the streets of a mirror image of Whitechapel London, as it would have looked in 1868.

Gaslights now illuminate the streets, revealing the form of a man slightly bent over, clinging to the sides of the house, with a dagger clutched in his hand, startled and frozen by the sudden light show.

"Well, that's different," mutters Dante from behind me.

Behind him, the man who'd been swinging his blade looks toward his prey and says to us, "Well, duckies, you seem to have caught us at a slight disadvantage, haven't you?" With a growl, he turns and flees back the way he'd come, leaving his comrade who'd been playing the victim to look nervously for a way to retreat.

Scuttling backward, he turns and runs after his partner. He doesn't get far.

Chapter 39

Swirling columns of mist land in the street, turning into people. A woman reaches out for the man who was playing decoy, grasps him by the shoulder, opens her mouth, and rips into his neck with her fangs. She only releases him once she's drained him. His limp body drops to the floor like forgotten rubbish.

In the distance, I hear taunting coming from the once shadow people, hunting the fleeing man, as he must have hunted them.

"I don't know how you did it, but thank you." The woman bows her head ever so slightly while staring at us with open curiosity. "Did you mean what you said?"

For a second, I wonder what she's talking about. My puzzlement must show because she releases a low throaty chuckle. "You look cute when uncertain, almost like a demented squirrel."

Instantly, I place my fingers over my nose to straighten out the scrunched look.

"I meant about what you said, about fighting *The Protectors*?"

"Yes. I did mean it."

"You truly believe you can finish them off?"

"Only with help," I reply, while watching her closely.

"To be free of them is a dream long prayed over; the reality, they are complex beings, more of a collective than an individual. I don't understand how they're formed." Shaking her head, she looks at us with pity, as if we're children she's about to tell heartbreaking news to.

"We've read the Prophecy, and we've also found out how they are so strong. They're linked through blood ties, which will be their undoing," I inform her. Taking a step closer, I watch her intently and see surprise in her eyes.

"You've found it? Who are you exactly? Vlasim is the keeper—"

"Vlasim? You know our sire?" demands Victor and Vincent who as one step forward, coming up on either side of me.

"Yes, of course, wait...your sire?" Turning to a man nearest to her, she tells him to hurry and pass the information along. In a flash, the man disappears, literally disappears by turning to mist and seeping away. Seriously cool, but creepy as hell.

"Well, that's different," mutters Dante.

"You do know you're saying that a lot, don't you?" Selene whispers back to him.

"What can I say," he answers with a smile in his voice. "I'm getting a serious eye-opener, and everything seems different."

A few minutes later, two shadows transform into people. I'm stunned to see Vlasim. Going by the gasps coming from either side of me, I'm not the only one.

"Sire? How can this be?" demand both vampires simultaneously.

"Shall we say, there was a certain female vampire I was surprised to see, who lured me into a trap?" Vlasim smiles slightly to take the sting out of his words, though

I notice that he does give Vincent a pitying look. "All this time you've been covering for her, you should have told us it wasn't you. We could have been there for you," he gently reprimands him.

"You don't blame me either?" Shock resonates in Vincent's voice and his face, and I notice his shoulders sag in surprise at the lack of blame.

"No, Vincent, you are not to blame for your mother's actions. I'm just glad it wasn't you," Vlasim replies, then gives him a stern look. "Though if you'd told us about her, I wouldn't have followed her into the trap. Now I have my body back, the next time I see her—"

"There won't be a next time," I interrupt him.

"What do you mean there won't be a next time? Nice to see you again. Shame you're dressed this time." He wags his eyebrows at me and smirks, which is quickly wiped off his face when he hears Victor growling in warning at him. "Ah, you two are…?"

"Yes," we answer together, though Victor's voice sounds like he's crunching rocks and spitting them out. I quickly explain to him, "Hecate sorted her out. Now about this coming war, we need your help."

The woman who'd summoned Vlasim looks in confusion at me, turning to him she asks, "Who is she?"

"My dear, she is the one from the Prophecies. The one with Double Magick." I hear reverence in his voice, and feel stunned at his seriousness.

"Truly?" Stepping forward, she quickly reaches out a trembling hand to me. "I can't believe you're real. I've always thought…"

"Thought what?"

"I'd assumed my sister was mistaken. After all, the

chances of your being here are so remote. Never mind that my niece's children would have survived."

"You're Janna's aunt?" Vincent demands, sounding as dumbfounded as I feel.

"You know Janna?" demands Vlasim, while her aunt stares at Vincent.

"She's my wife."

"Why isn't she here?" Staring over my shoulder, her eyes search my friends' faces as if Janna is hidden amongst them. Disappointment flashes across her face when she realizes she isn't there.

"She's with our daughter; they're both safe."

"Daughter?" A stunned silence echoes through the street after the whispered word spoken in reverent tones.

Janna's aunt nods her head at us, looks at her people, and with a huge smile on her face declares, "It's finally time to fight back. I never thought it would be possible, yet with Janna alive and a new generation born, let alone standing before us, and us." Waving her hand to encompass all the shadow people, she continues, "I can't believe my sister was right!" as if that's the most surprising aspect of everything.

Chapter 40

In my wildest dreams, I'd never imagine I'd be sitting around the kitchen table of what is Victor's house in our time, but is Janna's aunt's, Yvette's, home, in the Shadow World. But this is exactly what I'm doing. Drinking coffee and pondering over the decisions and actions that have brought us to this point.

When *The Protectors* decided to illuminate the Midnight Slasher, a rogue vampire on a killing spree, and failed, they unintentionally (I hope) ripped a hole in the ether and created the Shadowlands, where the dead rule, trapped in a nightmarish realm in 1868.

I can't help wondering where exactly the field of battle will be played out.

"I'm confused," I finally admit, turning to look at everyone. "Where exactly will this battle be fought? Hecate told us the battlefield has been chosen. But where is it?"

"Child, you know where it is; after all, you saw it happen, did you not?"

"Vlasim, I told you; it was a dream of one outcome of the war I saw."

"Yes, but that was the battlefield chosen, no matter what outcome plays out.

"Great, so who exactly is going to tell Prince of Wallachia Vlad Tepes that we're borrowing his land for a fight?" I ask, sarcasm dripping from each word.

"I think she should, just for speaking like that," Yvette informs the others.

I feel my eyes widen and hope like hell she's messing with me. I don't fancy broaching that particular question with Vlad, even though he was exceptionally helpful to us, and nice. The idea of asking for a favor of this magnitude…not something I'm dying to do, especially with his prior track record for impaling those who pissed him off. After all, he wasn't called the Impaler for nothing.

"It's okay, Candi; you won't have to ask him," Victor informs me. Taking hold of my hand, he informs me, "Vlad will be more than delighted to have his land used to kill *The Protectors,* and trust me when I say he's been looking forward to tearing them apart for a long, long time."

"Who did they kill that he loved?"

"What are the two main things you know about from all the stories about him?"

"His love and devotion to his wife who tragically killed herself, and that he was turned into a vampire before he could tell her."

"Vlad's wife was murdered by *The Protectors;* she didn't kill herself."

"What was she?"

"She was a vampire, and she is the one who turned him."

"Say that again? Wait, if she turned him, then why was she killed? That doesn't make sense." Waving my free hand, I almost hit Felicity in the face. "I mean, their killing never made sense, but this makes even less than normal."

"Do you remember in the stories about Vlad, that

wolves answered to him, and even in some stories he could turn into a wolf?"

"Yes…why?"

"Vlad was the alpha werewolf in his pack. Even once he was turned into a vampire, the wolves still obeyed him. No, he hasn't the ability to shapeshift anymore. Part of the fear of your being born was that if, no, *when* the Prophecy is realized, all magick will come back." Looking around at everyone, his eyes settle on Nancy. "Which means you for starters will once more be a necromancer, and a zombie."

"Fucking hell!" gasps Talia in awe, while staring wide-eyed first at Nancy before turning her gaze on me. "Feeling pressure yet?" she asks with a huge grin spreading across her face.

I can't help gaping at Victor. Reaching out, he places two fingers under my jaw and closes my mouth by gently pushing it closed, then strokes the side of my face.

"You'll be okay, sweetheart; we're in this together, no matter what."

Leaning forward, he brushes his mouth against mine, just the barest amount of pressure, yet the kiss ignites a fire deep inside me, flaring brightly. So for just a second, I feel as if I'm going to combust and soar into the sky, like a phoenix from the ashes. Opening my eyes, for just the briefest moment, I see flames and hear the screams of the dying.

"Come with me, Candi. There's something we must do now before the coming battle," Victor informs me while looking intently into my eyes.

With a nod of my head, I agree. I know exactly what he's on about, and he's right. I need to claim him properly as mine. But more than that, I want him to claim me as his. Hand in hand, we leave the others behind and enter the sitting room, closing the door firmly behind us.

We sit on the floor, facing each other, our legs crossed and knees touching. I take one of Victor's hands, place it over my heart, leaving mine on top. Victor does the same to mine.

With a trembling smile, I lean forwards, closing the distance between Victor and me. I feel the brush of his lips against my neck a moment before he sinks his fangs into me.

A contented sigh escapes me, and then I bite into his strong neck and finally through our link we say the words to claim each other.

"Victor Harlow, I claim you as mine, now and forever."

"Candi Reynolds, I accept your claim, and in return I claim you as mine, now and forever."

Our words spoken, we release each other from our bites, I'm just thinking I don't feel any different when gold threads of magick swirl around our bodies, entwining around us and linking us together in gentle bonds before seeping into our bodies. Gasping in a breath of wonder, I realize I can sense Victor's emotions. His love for me. Fear for all of us in the coming battle, and his hope for our future together.

"I accept your claim," I inform him, as I stare in wonder at the man before me.

Chapter 41

We gather once more at Vlad's castle. This time, though, Roísín and Janna are with us, and so are Nina, Vlasim, Yvette, and all the victims killed and cast into the Shadow World.

They fascinate me on some deep level, maybe because of the simple fact that they defied death, managing to survive in a way. Maybe because they can shift into shadow form, and yet they still have their supernatural abilities. Whatever the Shadow World was, it changed everyone who was trapped in it, making them…*more*.

It's only been a month since we were in Whitechapel, and apparently, they found a drummer, as the previous quiet is replaced with the sounds of a beating drum. The constant beat of it is driving me nuts; all I want to do is kill the drummer, just to stop the flipping noise.

Looking around, I stare in wonder at all that have been gathered together for the coming battle. I honestly don't know how they were summoned so quickly. After all, it's not as if we could advertise in the papers. A snort of laughter escapes me at the thought. I can just imagine what it'd read: "War starting at one o'clock, and don't forget your weapons."

Fear slides down my back as warriors sharpen their swords and knives. Some even add vicious needle-sharp finger guards to slice at the unfortunate person they'll be battling. I feel claustrophobic suddenly. My heart is pounding so fast, I'm surprised it hasn't jumped out of my chest and flopped away.

"Candi, sweetheart, come and take a walk with me."

Looking up I stare into Victor's eyes. My heart flips, and I can't help smiling up at him. *"You sensed my panic attack?"* I ask him telepathically. Ever since we claimed each other properly, our link has made us sensitive to each other's needs and able to communicate without speaking or being physically connected.

"Yes, my heart, I did. And no killing the drummer, unless it's the other side's. Though I must admit, the noise is grating on my last nerve too."

Linking hands with him, I allow him to pull me to my feet. Together, we move around the crowded room, avoiding stepping on people and their weapons.

Feeling eyes on me, I turn to stare directly at Vlad, who gives me an ever-so-slight bow of his head and a quirk of an eyebrow.

Letting down my mental barriers, I send my thoughts at him and allow him to reply. *"Sup?"*

"Really, Candi, my dear, you must learn to become more eloquent when talking." Laughter rumbles through his voice, and a small smile flickers across his mouth. *"You okay? Wherever you're going, don't be too long. This coming battle will be starting soon. The tempo of the drums has changed."*

"We'll be back soon. I promise. I just need…"

"I understand. Fear in a time like this is always good. It keeps you alive. Find me before the battle starts. And bring your companions with you. We'll all

fight side by side, for there is no one else I'd rather have at my back than you and your unusual group."

I incline my head at him, touch my index and middle fingers to my forehead, and then flick them to him, in a sign of respect and promise. Before I turn around, he returns my salute.

Chapter 42

Standing on the balcony, we look out over the masses splayed out before us. A hawk shifter returns from a scouting mission, flies over the parapet, and releases a sharp cry. Seeing us, he circles and descends to where we're standing.

Flashing into his human form, he looks at me with wide almond eyes. "Where is the Warrioress Daphmire Janna?" he demands. His throat bobs as he swallows, and his eyes flick back toward the enemy camp.

"What? She's in the—" Before I can say anything else, he places a large hand on my wrist interrupting my babble.

"Please, bring her here. I have news best not broken to her in front of others."

I glance at Victor and do the only thing I can think of, closing my eyes I connect with Vlad. *"Vlad, we need Janna up on the balcony facing the armies!"*

"Please, I need…"

"She's coming," I reply, interrupting the agitated shifter. Before he can say anything else, we hear a stampede coming up the stairs and bursting into the room behind us.

With Janna and Vlad in the lead, the rest of my friends are directly behind them.

"I only asked for the Warrioress Daphmire Janna, not everyone else," the hawk shifter mutters to me, though his eyes sparkle with mirth and a slight smile pulls at his mouth.

"Jonathan, what is it?" demands Janna, as worry flashes across her face upon seeing who has summoned her.

Moving forward, he grasps hold of her hands and bows his head to kiss her knuckles. "I bring news I never thought I would. Demetri is alive."

"What?" In horror, I watch as Janna sways slightly, her face losing all color and a tremble reverberates through her body.

Vincent pushes past a stunned Vlad, curls his arm around her waist, securing her to his side. Staring at the naked shifter in front of him, he growls out, "Are you sure?"

"Positive. I grew up with Janna and met him when she did."

"How can that be?" I ask, feeling completely floored by this news.

"Which, me growing up with Janna, or him being alive?"

"Well, both really, but how about the him being alive part first?"

"I don't know why he's alive, but if I have it my way, the bastard won't be for much longer," Jonathan growls, making us all gawp in shock at him. "He's their general!"

Chapter 43

A minute ago, I thought Janna looked like she was going to faint. Now, I think she could possibly explode, like a volcano. Her color returns as fury races across her face but gets brighter than usual.

"You lie!" she snarls, her eyes zero in on the hawk-shifter before her, as she reaches for her sword.

"Sweetheart, stop." Two little words and a hawk stays alive. Two little words and a warrioress collapses. The only thing keeping her on her feet is the man who loves her, who whispers soothingly to her until she finally straightens in his arms.

"I'm so sorry, but what I say is the truth. It is why I wanted to speak to you without all the other warriors watching."

"Are you sure?" I ask him, but seeing how devastated he is, I know the answer before he gives it.

"Yes. He's sitting on a white charger of all things. He saw me, and he laughed." Shaking his head, he looks completely baffled. "I don't understand why he laughed."

"He wanted you to know you definitely saw him," I reply. Receiving a startled look from him and Janna, I continue, "Don't you see? How do you get inside your enemy's head?"

"Is this some kind of riddle?" Jonathan inquires. He cocks his head to the side in such a bird-like fashion, if I didn't already know he was a bird shifter of some sort, I'd have guessed by that simple movement.

"No riddle, just the enemy playing a very clever game of war. Janna, did he know what you are, before you were together?"

"Yes, I think so? Why do you ask?"

"Because I'm wondering if—"

"If he targeted me for that reason, to be a spy in my camp, so to speak."

"Sorry, but yeah. Though you weren't a warrioress then, were you?"

"No, I became one afterward."

"Maybe he was turned during captivity?" I ask.

"Maybe," replies Janna, but the doubt in her voice is clear to all.

I take a deep breath, then look her directly in the eyes. I see her stand straighter, square her shoulders back, preparing herself for whatever I'm about to say.

"I believe he meant to kill you from the very beginning. You sent your son and daughter away for safety, yet there shouldn't have been anywhere safer than your mother's home, unless the enemy was already inside.

"Janna, you are the first Daphmire. A supernatural being who shouldn't exist. The first ever witch/vampire hybrid. An anomaly. A threat to *The Protectors* and a challenge to Demetri. I believe he wanted to kill you, but only once you evolved into a warrioress. An opponent worth fighting. Someone who could fight back. In his own way, I think he loved you; otherwise, he would have killed you before you trained in battle and became the Warrioress Daphmire, a worthy opponent and a woman who makes her enemies tremble in fear."

My words seem to hit her as if she's being pelted by rocks, and I can't help the twinge of guilt that washes through me at causing her further pain by mentioning her children she sent away so long ago and never saw again.

Her expression turns grim as does the others. With a nod of her head, she swivels out of Vincent's arms and marches forward toward the balcony.

For only she can rally those who knew her husband, for they had to be told that not only is he alive, but now, he's the enemy.

I indicate with my hand that we all should stand beside her, with Vincent on her right side and Vlasim, flanking her left. As a unit, we surround her. And in awe, I watch her not only rally our soldiers but make them bay for the blood of our enemies, and especially his.

And as I listen to them shout, I wonder if her ex-husband had murdered her previous lover, Hector. A man that brought a little happiness back into her life, after a century of pain and not knowing if Demetri was alive or dead.

I feel a warm hand take hold of mine and give it a reassuring squeeze. Glancing at Victor, I give him a small smile of reassurance and lean slightly into his side. Together, we listen to the bloodthirsty cries of our army and the thump of the drum as it beats in time with my heart.

As one, all of us on the balcony throw back our heads and roar our primal shouts into the sky. The war has officially begun.

Chapter 44

As one, we descend the stairs and march out into the clear cool spring day. Swords beat against shields. The drums beat in rhythm to our heartbeats and footfalls. Shifters transform into their animal forms. And the cry of the army reverberates with hope and vengeance.

Centering myself, I prepare for the pending battle. Calming my breathing, I reach out for my lover, friends, and my fellow warriors, connecting with each on a magickal thread so I won't harm them.

Bending, I touch the dirt, dig my fingers in, and pull the magick into me. As I rise up, threads of green earth magick cling between my fingers and the ground. Weaving my hands into the air, I reach for the air where white magick entwines with the green. Walking to the nearest camp fire, I bend once more, this time I reach into the heart of the fire.

Hearing gasps of surprise and shifting feet, I ignore everyone. Threads of the fire mix with the earth and air magick. Turning to a pan of water, I dip my fingers into it and join the fourth element to the other three. Green, white, red, and blue magick swirl and combine. Now all I need is the fifth element. Spirit.

I search the faces before me, until my gaze meets Victor's. A slight smile curls my lips as I open my heart for him to see and feel. I press my fingers against my chest and dig in slightly making myself bleed.

"What the hell is she doing?" someone mutters in a horrified whisper.

Violet and silver magick seep from my body and mix with the other elements. I raise my hands into the air, and my bleeding instantly stops.

I call out loud.

"Guardians of the Watchtower, I call unto thee…

"Earth." I draw a line in the sky. As green magick infused with the other elements appears, gasps of surprise sound, and everyone goes still.

"Fire." This time I draw a red line, connecting it to the last.

"Air." A white line joins the others, so I now have three quarters of a square.

"Water." The blue line completes the square, and it starts to vibrate.

"Join with me, Spirit." I put the silvery/violet magick in the center of the box and swirl it around with my finger. As spirit touches each of the elements, they once more fuse together, and as they expand and transform into a pentagram in the sky, the five elements grow larger and brighter, each line infused with all the colors.

"Goddess of the Underworld, hear my cry.

Goddess of the Crossroads, hear my call.

Goddess of the Witches, hear my plea.

Goddess of Magick, hear my wish.

Goddess Hecate, protector of us all.

I call unto thee, on this day of war.

Join with me and the Watchtower Guardians.

Join with us, those about to fight, against The Protectors."

The pentagram once more shimmers, though this time it twists in the air, as if on an invisible string. Twirling faster and faster until it shatters and sparks fly from it, and in its place Hecate and her hounds appear, hovering midair for just a second before drifting to stand firmly on the ground.

Everyone bows. Most kneel on the ground. Shock and awe reflect on most faces, though some have fear flickering too.

"On this day of war, all who shall fall will be remembered. The final battle is here, yet until the Prophecy is realized, your enemies won't fall completely." Hecate's words ring loud and clear across the field, allowing all our warriors to hear her words. Nervous looks are shared amongst them as fear flashes across their faces from her words.

"They will weaken, and they will crumble. And this will be the beginning of the end for them and their ways." She looks at all who are bowed before her; her eyes settle on everyone, and with an incline of her head she bows ever so slightly. *"Rise, warriors. Today is the day you've only dreamt of. The day most thought would never occur. This is the day you shall meet* The Protectors, *head on and with a battle cry.*

"This is the day you fight not just for your right to love and live life the way you're meant to, but for your descendants' rights too. It's time to release your fear and let your anger free and strike back against those who have hunted and killed for control and power, against you all!" Her words bellow from her as conviction and determination spread throughout the army. A cheer erupts, feet stamp, and the war trumpet blares.

Hecate and her hounds turn to mist and flow over everyone, a feather-light touch brushes against us as she passes. A blessing to each of us. And a promise of a better future. And most importantly of all, linking us all together, so none of us can harm each other with spells or weapons.

Chapter 45

Screams of the dying mix with the sounds of battle cries. Swords clash and scrape against metal and bone. Wolves howl, witches chant and cast spells, hawks screech their warnings, and horses trample those in their wake.

I twirl around in a half crouch, gathering power, and form a fireball which I shoot at my enemy. In the next instant, I shift to my wolf form, bound into the troops, and launch myself at my nearest prey.

His eyes widen in fear as my snarling mouth opens and snaps around his throat. Blood shoots into my mouth. Releasing him, I once more transform into my human form and fire more spells into the hordes before me.

A shout of warning echoes through the field, just before a man astride a white stallion charges off to my right. Turning my head, I notice Janna, her two swords appearing to be an extension of her, as she twists and turns with fluid grace, her swords hissing through the air as they slice through the enemy.

I blast a fireball into the horse and rider's path, causing the horse to rear up, his scream sounding shrill amongst the battle as his front hooves paw the air. A snarl emits from Demetri, as Janna turns in his direction. She flashes him a smile that would make most cower in fear. A look which promises vengeance.

Twirling in a circle with her arms crossed at shoulder height, her swords slice with deadly accuracy. I just have time to notice her do a sideways flip, her arms unwinding as she spins and chops at the ankles of those unfortunate enough to be caught in her path.

I circle my arm and draw magick to me, unleashing it in a magickal whip. Wrapping it around my enemies' necks, it cuts through them before they even know what happened. Running forward with my whip lassoing those in my way, I transform back into my wolf and attack. Bounding between ankles and bouncing onto backs, I leap into the fray.

A gap ripples through the ether, opening our world to the Shadow World. Arms reach through. Grabbing hold of a warrior, they drag him screaming through the portal. A moment later, more shadow spirits climb through the portal, fighting tooth and nail with our enemy and ripping them from our world into theirs.

Turning away, I spot Cedrix fighting alongside Rob Wiseman and the six ex-navy SEALs they both agreed to ask for help. Each man is fighting back to back with a sword and a hunting knife in their hands, while Jezebel in jaguar form circles them, lashing out and tackling any enemy unlucky enough to cross her path. Vivian in her werewolf form circles from the opposite side and charges at a huge man, who a moment later I realize is none other than Archibald Dight.

A mournful howl echoes through the fighting, catching my attention. Whipping around, I howl in return and dash through the field of blood and rage. Soon, I find the huge black wolf standing protectively over the fallen Alsatian.

Transforming back into my witch form, I kneel beside Jasmine. Blood mats her fur, and it takes me vital seconds to find the wound causing so much blood loss. Pressing my hands on her belly, I cringe as my fingers slip into her flesh, causing her to whimper in pain.

Breathing deeply, I filter my magick into a pin point and seal her skin back together. Her blood soaks back into her skin, and once more she's whole.

Rage flows through me as I see the fallen. My anger burns bright inside me, over the exhaustion on the faces around me, the desperation to survive this battle, and the pain of the wounds that have been inflicted.

I feel a shield slide down over my eyes, turning everything violet. My arms pulse. Glancing down, I am surprised to see them lit up like Christmas trees. The intricate web design now looks like a map, with bright pin points showing me where members of *The Protectors* fight. Granted, that's everywhere, yet there's something odd about how they're grouped together in some places. There's something I can't put my finger on.

Anger suddenly pulses through me. Gathering power to me, I twirl around in fury, bending and twisting in a strange dance, yet with each twist and dip, flames erupt around me, roaring into the sky, causing fear to ignite in the fighting warriors.

With a howl of rage, I once more transform into my wolf. Burning brightly, I run through the field leaping on all those I see on the map shining on my arms. Seeing Victor fighting for his life, I jump over a fallen warrior, twist midleap, and transform into my human form, landing behind my lover's enemy. I twist his neck and let the body drop to the ground.

Calling fire to my hands, I send the flames out. *"Follow the map on my arms, and extinguish only those from my enemy's camp."* Bright flames of silver, gold, and red rush from me, darting around the combatants, wrapping like steel bands around *The Protectors'* warriors, and with the slightest tightening, they drop to the ground. A quick death—they wouldn't even have known they were about to die.

The battle is over. All who had come to fight against us on this day are dead. And all that is left to do is heal our wounded. I send out healing magick which joins with the other witches around the battlefield. It slides over our wounded, cauterizing wounds and mending broken bones.

Sadness grips me at the deaths I've caused. Not the one on one fighting, but the final destruction. Murder, plain and simple. Tears cloud my vision. I look into the eyes of the man I love and whisper, "I'm sorry."

Transforming into my wolf, I howl mournfully my apology before darting off into the woods.

Chapter 46

I don't know for how long I ran; all I know is, by the time I stop running, I'm exhausted and darkness has fallen. My sides heaving from exertion, I collapse into foliage by a fallen dead tree. A shiver rakes through me, not from cold but the memories of the battle. The final moments when I'd murdered all those people in one brutal act of vengeance.

Transforming into my human form, I curl my body in on itself and wrap my arms around my knees. Tears flow unheeded down my face as I feel like my heart is breaking. I can't forgive myself for the atrocities I've just committed.

I'll rest for a while and then move on. I can't face the others, and yet the thought of never seeing my friends again hurts me, but not as much as the thought of being without Victor. The only man I've ever loved. My soul mate.

I howl out my agony causing birds to take flight with squawks of irritation and wildlife to scatter. I repeat a litany of an apology over and over, as if this will somehow release me from my guilt or change what I did.

I loosen the grip I have on my legs and let them slip to the side. "I'll have to keep moving. I can't let anyone find me," I mutter out loud, as if to hear the words will encourage me to get up and go.

"You want to keep moving because otherwise you'll know no one will come looking for you."

My fear whispers in a snide voice, telling me the truth of my deepest fears.

"You did them a favor running away, saved them from driving you out. After all, you're a vindictive monster!"

It's only when I wipe away my tears and prepare to stand that I realize I'm not alone. And it wasn't my voice in my head I was hearing. I should have realized, as now I think about it, it was a man's voice I'd heard.

Staring balefully at me with a knife clutched in his palm, he curls his lip at me in disgust. "You're a disgrace to her memory. I should have killed you long ago."

"Who are you?" I demand. "And a disgrace to who's memory?"

"Cynthia's, of course. Who else would I be on about?" the man asks me in such a tone of voice you'd think it was a logical assumption.

"I don't know you, so how the hell would I know who you're on—wait, you knew my mother?"

"Of course I knew her. I loved her!" bellows the man. Rage flashes across his face as his grip tightens around the handle of the knife. He advances a step closer to me, then pauses, his head tilted as if listening to something farther away.

"Who are you?" I ask again, slowly I stand up.

Once more, he focuses on me, glowers at seeing me standing up. "You look so much like her. Seeing you is like seeing her alive again." His tone is filled with regret, looking at me, he curls his lip up in a snarl of anger.

"I'm Jeremy Reynolds, and I should have been your father, by rights. Except she never looked at me the way she looked at Killian. The moment they clapped eyes on each other…I ended up hating him, my own brother. Do you know what that's like? To hate your own…"

I gape at him. This man who hates me for looking like my mother. Who hated his own brother because my mother loved him; this man is my uncle? I stare at him in shock. I feel as if I'm watching a train crash and can't look away.

Lifting my hand to drag my hair away from my face, I notice a blip on my arm. I'm horrified as I realize that my own uncle must be a member of *The Protectors.*

"You're one of them." I don't ask him if he is, because the evidence is in front of me. I stare at him in disgust. *How could he join them after what they did to his own brother and the woman he supposedly loved?*

"Of course I'm one of them," he shouts. Spittle flies from his lips, spraying everywhere. "I needed permission to kill Killian. By the time I joined them long enough to hunt, they'd married and she was pregnant with you!"

I feel myself go icy cold at his words. I stare at this stranger who's apparently my uncle. A man who joined a group of maniacs because my mother didn't love him. A man who killed his own brother and the woman they both loved. My mother.

"You joined them so you could kill your brother?" I hope I've somehow managed to get the wrong idea.

"Of course I did. What was I supposed to do, wish them happy?"

I stare at him blankly wondering if he actually hears himself. "Yes." Shaking my head, I stare at him in disbelief.

"Don't be stupid!"

"Who killed my parents?" I ask the only question that is now relevant. The only question I've ever wanted to know the answer to.

****

I stare sightlessly out my sister's apartment window, as turmoil flows through me. My thoughts are haunting me, and it's only my sister's strident voice that pulls me out of my internal battle. Though to be honest, her words are not what I need, or want to hear.

"You are obsessed, just as our father was obsessed with her mother. What is it about those women that have the men in our family tying themselves up in knots over them?" demands Sophie, in genuine confusion.

"You don't understand." I cringe as I hear the petulant tone in my voice.

"You're right; I don't. What I know is another matter altogether, though. Our father hated Killian, his own brother, because he wanted Cynthia for himself. Even though it was obvious from the first time Killian and Cynthia met that they'd fallen in love with each other and had no eyes for anyone else."

"How do you know this?" Turning, I stare curiously at my sister. "Neither of us was even born when they all met..."

"Mum was there. They all went to college together. She was dating Dad at the time, and she told me about it. She remembers how Dad became moody and acted jealous every time he saw them together. She almost broke up with him over it."

"So how come she didn't?"

"She fell pregnant." Waving a hand to shush me before I can point out that I wasn't old enough, she continues on, *"Not with you, she miscarried soon after, and Dad became attentive around her. Not long after that though, Killian asked Cynthia to marry him, and she accepted.*

"Dad was furious. It wasn't long afterward that he became secretive." Pausing in her story, she turns away to look out the window. *"He asked Mum to marry him, she said yes because she loved him, but she admitted to me, she always felt like she was second best. Not long after they'd married, she realized that he'd joined* The Protectors.*"*

"He joined because he was jealous that he didn't marry Cynthia?"

"Yes. He wanted her. I half think he decided to kill them so that no one could have her, including Killian, his own brother."

"Jesus. I never knew. Why didn't Mum tell me?" I feel anger and confusion wash through me and hurt, too.

"Because, Mark, she knew how close you and Dad were, and Dad..." Shaking her head, she turns to once more look at me. *"Do you honestly believe he would have let her tell you the truth of why he'd joined* The Protectors*? He was grooming you to follow in his footsteps, which you did, in more ways than one.*

"Why you are so obsessed with our cousin, I'll never know. But for your own sanity, you must stop this foolishness. Warn her of the danger she's in. After all, our own father is more than willing to kill her, just to eradicate the final link to Cynthia's memory."

I can feel my face paling at the thought of harm coming to her. I hate the idea of her being with that vampire or, truth be told, with anyone. But the thought of her being in danger leaves me in a cold sweat.

I know my sister doesn't understand my obsession with our cousin. How could she? After all, I've never told anyone, that each night, Candi's screams echo in my sleep. I'm haunted by her heartbreak and rage. Emotions I helped to cause.

"If she survived the battle, I'll warn her about Father."

"The battle, why wasn't he fighting in it? I'd have thought that would have been right up his street."

"He's not needed for the battle; he's a tracker, one of the best and too valuable to be killed in the war." Looking at my sister, I admit, "We both were on the no-fighting list. Only half of each level was allowed to fight." Shaking my head, I wonder if Candi will survive, and for the first time ever, I hope that her friends and lover will also live.

****

"My son and I did. Your father was his first hunt. You should have seen his expression when he realized I was going to kill him." A satisfied smirk slithers across his face, as he twirls his knife around in his hands.

"Cynthia should have died then too, except my wife went into labor. Took me three fucking years to track her down again. When she realized it was me…" Sorrow for just an instant enters his eyes, before they harden once more. "I asked her to come with me; she refused. Said she couldn't stand the sight of me, and blah, blah, blah, how could I do this to my brother and wife?"

I feel a brush of familiar power vibrate through me. It's the only warning I have before Jeremy's neck twists around at an unhuman angle and drops to the ground. Standing staring at me is Victor Harlow, vampire most scrumptious and the love of my life.

Chapter 47

"No matter what," Victor growls, as he stalks toward me.

"What?" I ask in confusion, as I watch him close the distance between us.

"You promised, no matter what, we're in this together," he slowly enunciates, as if explaining to a rather dimwitted child.

"Yes, but—"

"No buts. No-matter-what does not have an escape clause!"

"Please, after what I just did—"

"You saved us all." His expression and tone become soothing, his eyes filled with sympathy.

"I murdered thousands!" I scream at him, shocking myself at the sudden volume in my voice.

"Sweetheart, it was a war. If you hadn't done…if you hadn't used your magick to end it swiftly, we would all have been dead."

"I didn't give them a chance to fight or even surrender…I just…" Tears fill my eyes once more, my body trembles, and it's suddenly very hard to swallow.

Arms wrap around me, holding me against his solid chest, as he strokes my hair and murmurs soothing noises in my ear. It takes me a while to realize he's repeating the same sentence over and over. "You saved us all."

Chapter 48

I must have collapsed from exhaustion because I'm not in the woods anymore. Instead, I'm in a bed, held securely in his arms, with one of his legs thrown over mine as if to make sure I'm pinned in place and can't disappear on him again.

Looking around as far as I can, it only takes me a moment to realize we're in our bedroom at Vlad's castle. What gives me pause, though, is the fact that we're both fully dressed. This fact makes me realize just how much I hurt him. As previously, no matter how tired I've been, awake or not, he would always undress me, leaving me in my underwear but needing that skin-to-skin contact.

I try to wiggle my arms free, from where they're trapped at my sides but am unable to as Victor has me pinned to him good and tight. I quickly realize that the only thing I can move is my head. Not good as I desperately need the toilet.

"Victor, Victor, wake up!" I call out. He shifts slightly, dragging me even closer to him, though I have no idea how. "Wake up." My voice has a tinge of desperation in it.

"I'm never letting you go again," mumbles Victor in such a sleepy voice I wonder if he's even awake.

"I need to pee," I growl at him. "Wake up, you oaf!"

"Did you just call me an oaf?" His voice has a hint of puzzlement in it and sounds just a little more awake than before.

"Yes, I did, and if you won't let me up, it'll become very uncomfortable in a minute."

Slowly, he releases me, as if unsure if he should. I feel his eyes drilling holes into my back as he watches me get up and head toward the bathroom. I practically run in, unbuttoning my jeans as I go and make it just in time.

Once I've finished, I enter the bedroom to find Victor pacing the floor. His brow is furrowed, and his normally elegant and fluid movements are stilted. For some reason, I find this quite distressing, knowing that I have caused this anxiety in him.

"I'm sorry." Shaking my head, I pause in the doorframe, unsure what to do. I don't feel like I have a right to go to him, to offer comfort. Lord only knows I can't give him any reassurances.

He pauses to stare at me. His hands ball up into fists before he slowly straightens them out one finger at a time. His jaw is working, and I know he's grinding his teeth. So not good. But it's his eyes that make me pause, and a cold sweat breaks out over my body as I stare into his vampiric icy blue eyes with a red ring swirling around them. I've never seen anything like it before.

I have a moment of panic where I debate stepping back into the bathroom and locking the door behind me. It's only his precise, single word sentences spoken with such deadly command that stop me from doing just that.

"Don't. You. Dare."

Swallowing, I give him the barest nod, letting him

know I won't run.

"Strip."

"What?" I ask, feeling I must have misunderstood him, because surely he didn't just—

"I said, strip!" He takes a step toward me, and I'm positive he looks like he's expanding.

"Now look here—"

"I am going to make sure you don't run away again, and the only way I can think to stop you at this moment is if you're fucking naked!" His words are fired at me, each louder than the last until he's bellowing.

I shake my head in denial. "No, I won't."

"Won't what? Strip or run again?" He looks me up and down with lips curled into a snarl, yet I see just a glimpse of vulnerability in his eyes. The barest flash before being soundly squashed.

"Both. Look, I'm not going anywhere." I glance down at the floor and take a couple of minutes to just try and sort out my thoughts. "You have to understand, I didn't want to leave you." Taking a deep breath, I continue to explain what I was feeling, am still feeling to be honest. "How can I expect you to even look at me, if I can't, because of what I did?"

Confusion clouds his face at my words. In an instant, he's standing in front of me, looking torn between the idea of shaking me, strangling me, or hugging me. Apparently, he decided on two out of the three, by first shaking me by the shoulders before embracing me.

"Oh, Candi, what am I going to do with you?" He suddenly goes very still. I lean back slightly so I can look at his face.

For some strange reason, he looks as if he's been hit over the head with a shovel and is completely stunned senseless. His eyes have widened so much that they look as if they're about to take over his face. Thankfully, the freaky red in his eyes has gone.

"Are you okay?" I ask, feeling very worried that the answer might be a no. I watch him blink a couple of times and almost see the exact moment he comes to some conclusion or another.

Looking down at me, he glides his hands down my back and over my wrists to take hold of my hands. Slowly, he walks backward, bringing me with him until he reaches the bed. Sitting down on the edge of it, he tugs me slightly until I'm sitting beside him. Releasing one of my hands, he grasps me gently by the chin, holding me firmly so I'm looking him directly in the eyes.

"What did you feel just before you cast your last spell on the battlefield?"

I feel my back instantly stiffening. I try to jerk my chin out of his grip, but his hold is tighter than I thought, and his hand holding mine tightens.

"Answer the question, please. What did you feel just before—"

"I heard your question," I snarl at him. "I felt... hopeless, terrified, as if we were all about to die, and I felt so much rage and anger." Tears fill up my vision, my nose feels clogged up, and I really, really want to be alone right now so I can cry.

"That's because we were all about to die, Candi."

"What?" I stare at him as if he's suddenly speaking a new language that I can't understand. "What are you on about?"

"They were about to kill us all. They were gathering together in certain areas of the field where they could safely work together to kill us all at once. Even their own warriors were classified as expendable."

"I don't get it. How were they going to kill us all, and are you serious—they were going to kill their own too?"

"A mixture of fey and witch magic, added in with gunpowder, mixed into a cannon ball which they were about to fire on us.

"If you hadn't sent your magick out the way you did, we would all have been dead. When I told you, you saved us all. I meant it. Literally."

"They were gathering in groups?" I ask, thinking back to when I saw the weird clusters of *The Protectors* on my arms and being unable to figure out why it looked so odd. *Because they weren't gathered where the fighting was.*

"Even so, I still…"

"Feeling guilty is a good thing. It means you have remorse and a conscience. Sweetheart, if I could have done what you did, so that you wouldn't have this guilt eating away at you, I would. In a heartbeat." Leaning closer to me, he kisses me on the forehead. I can't help my eyes closing at the gentleness of the action.

My heart feels a little lighter, relief easing me slightly over the fact that my actions had saved everyone—well, except for the opposite side. Still, what was it that had made me realize I needed to take that particular and rather devastating course of action?

The strange groups on your tattoos…they were what caught your attention. But was it just my attention that was caught? I'd connected with the Guardians of the Watchtower and Hecate. They were able to see through me. Could...?

"Victor...?"

"What is it, sweetheart?" With the hand that was holding my chin, he strokes the side of my face, before dropping his hand to take mine in his once again.

"I healed Jasmine, and then my vision went strange..."

"Strange how, exactly?" His brow furrows as he stares in puzzlement at me.

"It was weird, as if a shield had slid over my eyes, and everything turned violet and sharp, ever so sharp. My tattoos also showed me exactly where all members of *The Protectors* were. I remember being puzzled over their strange groupings on the outskirts of the battlefield.

"Do you reckon...do you reckon the Guardians of the Watchtower and Hecate could have been seeing through my eyes?"

"I don't know. I mean, you did call them to help fight. Could they not have used you as their weapon? Why don't you ask them?"

I stare at him in surprise. I hadn't thought of asking them. Even though the decision was mine, and the choice was mine too. If they'd been seeing through my eyes, they might have realized what was happening and allowed me to sense the danger we were in.

Ultimately, the choice was mine, with or without their knowledge of how great the danger. So, does it matter? Would knowing they could sense what was going on around us and that maybe, just maybe, I was allowed to peek into the danger, would it change anything? No. It changes nothing. My actions, after all, are mine. I've accepted that fact; now I need to learn to live with them.

"Candi, I'm going to say this to you one more time. And this time I really need you to listen. You saved us all." He pauses to allow those words to sink in to me. To realize exactly what they mean with the new knowledge of what I did.

I take a deep breath and then give the slightest inclination of my head, letting him know I'm listening.

"And no matter what, we, as in you and I, are in this together. I love you, and I've already told you, I will never let you go. I am yours, and you, dammit, are most definitely mine."

"You are persistent. I'll give you that." A chuckle escapes me, surprising me, more for the fact that I didn't think I'd be able to laugh again, or have the right to do so. Yet the simple sound eases a tightness deep inside me, and I know, eventually, I will be okay.

****

My heart pounding like crazy, I sit up in bed. As the sweat-riddled blankets trap my legs, all I feel is fear, so much fear. For just a moment, my sleep-addled brain screams out a warning as the confusion of the terror I feel slithers down my spine like icy fingers.

It takes me a moment to realize the emotions I'm feeling aren't mine, and another moment before I understand where they're coming from. The emotions are from those members of The Protectors in my blood link. This can only mean one thing. Somehow, Candi survived the battle. Somehow, my cousin and those fighting alongside her defeated everyone. But how?

Shucking off the blankets, I scramble from the bed. Letting my hand reach out, I pat the air in search for the bedside lamp, and once my hand connects with it, I switch it on, bringing light into the darkness. A snort of hysterical laughter escapes me at the irony of the situation. The might of The Protectors sweeping across the world devouring all those in its path and one woman literally brings them trembling to their knees.

"She is the ultimate light in the darkness we've brought to our people," *I mutter out loud. Glancing around my sister's spare room, I can't help wondering, once I leave, will I ever see her again, or will this be my final goodbye? Sadness swamps me, almost drowning me in the emotion. What would my life be like if I hadn't followed my father on his path to madness? Would I have married, been happy, lived a proper life even if it wasn't...wasn't what, filled with death and regrets? What's the point in wondering, when it doesn't matter anyway? I made my choice, reveled in the deaths, all except...*

Shaking my head at the folly of my thoughts, I gather my clothes and head for the shower. It's time to face my destiny. Time to return to Paradise Falls where she'll eventually return too, and when she does... Pausing from collecting my jeans from where I'd dropped them on the floor last night, I realize I honestly don't know how to finish that train of thought.

Slowly, I gather my things and prepare myself for saying goodbye to my sister, the one person who always knew the real me, even when I didn't.

Chapter 49

A week has gone by since the battle. Those who'd survived the battle and were injured are recovering. Jasmine has only started to move about, as her wound has caused her a great deal of pain. Kheda hasn't left her side for the week, except for bathroom breaks, and only then because he couldn't take her with him.

We're still at Vlad's castle, and I'm slowly going crazy. I need space. I need to run. Not run away, just run. I'm beginning to feel cornered, and I don't like it. Everyone has been watching me. No matter where I turn, I bump into someone, who then gives me this wide-eyed look of…something. I can't put my finger on it, but it annoys the shit out of me. Mind you, everything is grating on my nerves at this stage.

I need to run. To just breathe in and out without feeling…hurt. Sad. Guilty. And I can't do that by being watched. My mind has gone into a tailspin of emotions. Anger and sadness over my grandmother's actions. Heartache from finally knowing why my parents were killed, and by whom, yet fury over the stupid reason that tore my family apart and brought about my grandmother's actions. And finally, relief that my uncle, the man that set everything in motion with his jealousy, is dead. And gratitude that Victor killed him, because honestly, I don't think I could have.

So much has been revealed in such a short time. I

finally know who killed my parents and why. The knowledge has both released a deep pain inside me but also left me feeling so confused. How can someone declare to love another, yet willingly cause them so much pain and even death?

Which in turn makes me think of my grandmother. A woman who loved me but became power hungry, and was going to kill me but didn't. Thinking of her makes me feel so confused, and I wonder, could I ever trust her enough again to let her back into my life? After all, even though she opted to not kill me herself, she didn't try and save me either.

A sense of urgency flows over me, and I know that if I don't go now, I'll never be "right" again. I won't be able to shake this dark cloud crushing me. Before I can change my mind, I write Victor a quick note, letting him know I will be back soon.

My dearest Victor,

You are the love of my life, my other half, my soul mate. I'll be only gone a short while. I'm just heading out for a run. So please don't worry if I'm not here when you read this. Though to be honest, I'll probably be back before you do.

I have a feeling deep inside that if I don't go now, I'll never be okay again. We'll never be okay or able to move forward with our lives, together. I hope you know how much I love and need you. You are my heart, my destiny, my everything. Yours forever and all eternity.

Candi

P.S. I'll be back in time for dinner at the very latest.

I feel slightly giddy after writing the letter, as I definitely know I am going outside on my own. I quickly put on my trainers, and with a final glance around the room, I descend the stairs and exit the front door without seeing anyone.

I stand outside for just a second breathing in the scents. I realize this was a bad mistake as the smell of death and blood assail my senses. It'll take a long time for that scent to disappear, though the memory of what happened will cling to the earth.

Turning in the opposite direction, I jog into the woods, following the path that we took the last time we were here. Strange how long ago that feels even though it was a scant few months since the New Year's Ball.

I run down the path. Ducking low-hanging branches, I let my feet pound on the dirt path, snapping broken twigs lying in my path. The wind tickles my face and brushes my hair out of my way, and I finally feel a small smile curl my lips upward.

I pump my arms and legs faster and run farther down the path than I've previously been. My heart beats at a steady pace, and I feel, for the first time in a week, alive. I can't help the laugh that gurgles out from me, the sense of joy I finally feel, and the knowing that I am alive. I shout out into the woods a simple hello, and then I see it. Standing in the middle of the path, staring intently at me.

Chapter 50

I stumble and skid to an unsteady stop, almost tripping over my own momentum and the branches on the path. Until finally I stop, panting in great gulps of air, to stare wide eyed at the wolf in the road. The same wolf I'd seen the last time I traveled this path, and I wonder if Jezebel is right and this is my spirit animal.

"Hello," I whisper to it, unsure if I should talk to it or if I'm meant to wait and see if it does something first.

The wolf cocks its head to the side, watching me intently, finally it chuffs out what sounds like a laugh and comes closer to me.

"You've been doubting yourself and in pain. Why?"

It takes me a moment to realize it's the wolf that's talking to me. Speaking directly into my head. I sit down on the road, facing the wolf who sits directly in front of me.

"Because of what I did."

"Yet you were told that your actions saved everyone, still you doubt yourself. Why?"

I feel frustrated with this conversation and wonder for a split second if Victor has managed to transform into a wolf. Shaking my head at the idea, I concentrate instead on the question.

"Because when I acted, I didn't know if my actions

would save us too. I killed all those people because I was angry and terrified we'd all die."

"Do you not wonder that this could have been because you sensed the truth in your feelings? You are more than just a witch. You have been destined to save lives and return all magicks.

"To do this, sometimes you also have to destroy and take away the lives of your enemies. No easy task, I must admit, yet you have been chosen because you feel. You are the Witness Who Feels. The Double Magick one. And eventually you will have another title. What that is, I cannot yet tell you."

I can't help it. I gape at the wolf, who gives me such an amused look before bumping his snout against mine in a friendly gesture.

"Stop running from your fate. Return to your soul mate. It's time for the next chapter of your destiny to begin. A destiny you and your vampire will partake in together." The wolf lowers his head at me as if bowing, stands up, and simply disappears.

"Return to him" is the final thing I hear whispered on the breeze before I stand up and run back the way I'd come. I need to see Victor and tell him what happened. A smile spreads across my face, and my heart feels lighter than it has in a while.

Chapter 51

I dash back to the castle. Flinging open the door, I shout out, "Victor?" and am surprised to hear a groan from behind me.

"Right here, sweetheart. You almost pummeled me through the wall with the door."

Turning around so fast I almost go skidding, I launch myself at him and knock him into the wall, before kissing him soundly.

Once our mouths unlock, he releases a chuckle. Leaning his forehead against mine, he looks me in the eye with a silly grin on his face. "I take it your run did you a world of good. God, I've missed you."

Pulling back slightly, I stare at him in confusion. "I've been right here. How could you miss me?"

"Candi…" Shaking his head at me, he looks for an instant so sad I want to cry and ease his hurt. "You might have been physically here but not emotionally. You've been trapped in emotional guilt and pain, unwilling or unable to release yourself from it."

Leaning forward, I kiss him gently on the mouth. A more brushing of our lips than anything. "I'm sorry I hurt you. I didn't mean to. I have something to tell you, though." Taking a step backward, I link my fingers with his and drag him toward the stairs and ultimately our chamber.

Once inside, he sits on the bed with his back

against the headboard. I don't sit down; I can't. Instead, I pace the length of the room, backward and forward, letting the words flow from me with each step I take.

I quickly tell him of what I was feeling before going for the run, the sense of urgency and desperate need and mainly the knowledge if I didn't go straight away, I would never be able to disentangle myself from the pain of my actions.

And then I tell him how I felt when I was running, up until seeing the wolf and the conversation that came about with my spirit animal.

Once done, I sit beside him and curl up next to him. His arms wrap around my waist and my head rests on his shoulder. Finally, I feel at peace.

Closing my eyes, I relax into the strength of Victor's body. I feel his hand caressing me from shoulder to hip and back again. With each stroke of his hand, I feel a little bit more healed inside, as if his touch is literally filling the gaps in my soul that have been ripped apart.

A puff of air escapes me, and in that moment, I feel once more complete.

Chapter 52

Leaning down slightly, he kisses me. I reach up and wrap an arm around the back of his neck and deepen the kiss. I nip at his bottom lip, and once he parts his lips, my tongue dives into his mouth to tangle with his.

A groan of satisfaction emits from us. I'm not sure who made the noise; maybe we both did. All I know is I feel sparks shooting through my system, bringing life back to what felt like it would be cold and dead forever.

My spare hand grasps his shoulder, as I move myself onto his lap to straddle him. My hands massage his hair and shoulder as I grind myself into his lap. His arousal pulses hard between us, and I feel it jumping slightly between my legs. A hiss of satisfaction leaves me at the feel of him rubbing against me.

"Too many clothes," I mutter into his mouth.

"Are you sure?" he asks, pulling his head back ever so slightly, just enough to make eye contact. I see the hunger flaring in his eyes, mixed with the desire echoing in his voice.

"Very," I purr, as I lean closer to once more claim his mouth with mine. I grasp the bottom of my t-shirt with both hands and pull it up, releasing my mouth from his long enough to get my top over my head before fusing my lips back to his.

His hands run over my torso, kneading and

stroking it, as our tongues mate and withdraw from each other. I run my fingers through his soft hair, down his back, and up the inside of his t-shirt. I need skin-to-skin contact. With a growl of frustration, I tug his top upward and receive a masculine chuckle of amusement for my trouble.

"Allow me." On these amused words, he rips his top up the middle, exposing his muscular chest to my eager eyes, mouth, and hands.

He wraps his arms around my waist, trapping my hands against his body as he pulls me tight against him, only to lean forward to tip us over, me on the bottom with him secured between my legs.

With a wicked smirk, he grinds his pelvis into mine, grips the waist of my tracksuit bottoms, and hooks his fingers into them and my panties before pulling both down and pulling away from me to remove them, my trainers, and socks in one swift movement.

I suddenly feel extremely naked, and not just because I am. I'm open to him completely, both my body and my heart. Before I can close my legs, he grips my knees and, with the barest shake of his head, spreads them wider.

"Never hide from me, Candi." Victor's voice rumbles from his chest, sounding like a large cat purring as milk chocolate melts in its mouth. His eyes are passion-filled vampiric blue fire, and his fangs are descended and look exactly what they are, very shiny deadly weapons that can be oh so sensual too.

Lifting my legs, he places them on his shoulders, bends down, and takes a long lick up my leg toward the center of my body. For some strange reason, this reminds me of something.

"Victor, stop," I moan. I receive an arched eyebrow and an are-you-kidding-me look for my trouble. "No, seriously, I was out running; I need to go and shower," I splutter in complete mortification. *How the hell did I forget I was all sweaty and yucky?*

"No."

"No what?" I demand in utter confusion as I pause from trying to swing myself around and off the bed. Clamping one large hand squarely in the middle of my chest, he easily prevents me from moving. But to my complete mortification, while he holds my upper torso still, my legs go flapping about the place.

"No, I won't stop." He chuckles evilly at my obvious discomfort. "Don't worry, sweetheart, I'll have you forgetting you want a shower soon.

"I doubt that very...Ohhh!" My back bows off the bed, and my eyes almost check out the back of my skull when his lips clamp down on my nub, gently sucking it, before his tongue pushes between my labia and licks a path up to my center before diving in.

Before long, my body starts to vibrate and tremble. My fingers scrabble for a handhold and don't seem to be able to grasp onto anything. I keep repeating the words "oh, oh God" over and over, as if I can't say anything else. Probably because I can't. Everything in my body becomes heightened and more sensitive, building into a climax, until finally it washes over me and releases. My toes curl, my back bows off the bed, and my breasts heave as if I've run a marathon. I scream my release and pleasure into the room until my voice goes hoarse. Just when I feel it easing, Victor tweaks my nipples causing more stimulation to vibrate through me.

Lifting his head up, his lips glistening from my release, he climbs up my body and kisses me. He claims me with his mouth and body. With one hand on his penis, he positions himself at my entrance, before burying himself inside me with one powerful thrust.

A groan of satisfaction rumbles from him as my inner muscles clamp around him. Slowly, he withdraws from me, leaving only the tip of his head inside before slamming back into me, swivels his hips, and repeats.

Our tongues fuse together, mimicking our bodies' movements. I lift my hips up off the bed meeting him with every thrust and deepening his penetration. Wrapping my legs around his shoulders, he shifts to a kneeling position and sucks on one of my nipples while squeezing and flicking the other.

My hands explore his hair, shoulders, and everywhere I can reach, before inching between our bodies and cupping and fondling his swinging balls every time they come my way. A growl reverberates from him, as he pounds harder into me. His hips swivel before retreating once more.

"Damn it, I can't get enough of you," he mutters into my ear, right before he sucks on my earlobe and gently nips it.

"Good," I purr in reply. My breathing is uneven and saying that one word feels like an accomplishment. I feel the beginnings of another orgasm spreading through me. I lower my legs from his shoulders to his hips and push onto my elbows, forcing him to sit up straighter and wrap one arm around my waist while leaning on the other.

Arching my back, I thrust and rotate my hips, speeding up as I feel my release flowing closer, faster.

Until finally with a scream of completion, I rock into him one more time, wrap my arm around his neck, and bite into him, drinking the blood that escapes him, as I feel his fangs descend into me, muffling his roar of satisfaction, as he drinks his fill and ejaculates inside me.

We pause as if frozen in shock when we hear the distinct sound of a heartbeat thumping four times. Ba-dum, ba-dum, ba-dum, ba-dum, coming not from me, but Victor.

Withdrawing our mouths from each other's necks, we stare in confusion at one another. Placing a hand over his chest, I feel his heartbeat thumping beneath my palm three more times before it stops once more.

"Holy shit!" I exclaim in surprise as I stare wide-eyed into his just as shocked-looking gaze. "Has that ever happened before?"

Shaking his head in denial, he opens and closes his mouth for a bit until finally a croak comes out. Clearing his throat, he tries again and a strangled, "No," emerges.

"Well, fuck me sideways. That was different," I mutter in awe, at which I receive a lascivious grin.

"I'll happily comply, but yeah, that was definitely different." Slowly, he backs out of me, and as he slides from my body, we stare in bafflement at the traces of his semen, which, normally a pale pink, is now most definitely white. Just as it would be from a live human.

"Bloody hell," I whisper, my eyes look up to meet his for a fleeting second before his gaze drops down to my belly.

"Do you think…" he asks as he reaches out to lay a large hand on my stomach, "we could have just got you pregnant?"

I open my mouth and close it again. My gaze drops to where his hand lies possessively on my stomach, gently stroking my skin. Shaking my head, I finally admit in a quiet voice, "I don't know. Maybe?"

"If we have, then the Prophecy could be coming true."

I stare at him in surprise. I don't know what to say to be honest. The words I read from the Prophecy swirl around my brain as if they're being spoken directly to me.

And the Double Magick one will be born stronger than any other.

Gather unto thyself allies to fight in preparation of the coming of the Triple Magick one.

When the Double Magick one fails to rise again, there will be two Triple Magick ones, to end the battle against the supernaturals' enemies.

For as The Protectors *meld their blood, making all one, the Triple Magick ones shall destroy them all with one swift pulse.*

And once more all races shall live in freedom and love as all magicks will grow once more.

Could this mean I'm the mother of the Triple Magick one? And if so, what exactly does it all mean?

Chapter 53

"I don't understand. What exactly does it all mean?" Flinging my hands up in the air as if I'm hoping that the answers will fall from above, I resume pacing the bedroom, where I'm surprised I haven't worn a path into the carpet.

"Candi, come and sit down," instructs Victor from where he's been watching me from the bed.

His expression is one of concern and hope, though he's also looking a little aggravated too. It could have something to do with me almost throwing him out of the way in my dash to get off the bed to pace so I can sort out my thoughts. Not that it's helped. At all. Instead, I feel more uncertain and scared.

Every time my gaze slides toward the bed and I see that damp spot, my eyes shy away and my need to pace increases. Until I finally swing around to face him, open my mouth and nothing. No words come out, not even a croak. Nothing.

My shoulders sag, tears fill up my eyes, and I make to run to him. Instead, he's just there, his arms wrapped around me, holding me tight as he makes soothing shushing noises. That's when I realize I'm bawling my heart out.

"It'll be okay. We don't even know if you are, sweetheart." His soothing words finally penetrate my brain. I sniffle and pull back slightly so I can see his face.

"But I want to be," I admit in a hiccupping voice.

Gently, he wipes my tears from my face. His gaze when it connects with mine is one of love and devotion, and my heart flutters, actually flutters in delight.

"I hope you are too. The idea of having a family with you is more than I ever could dream or wish for. I love you, and I need you in my life." A slight smile curves his full lips upward, yet his gaze is steady and intense as he watches me.

"I know we've claimed each other, but I want more. I want the world to know you're mine. Candi." Suddenly, he drops to one knee, and I just gape at him in all his naked glory. "Will you marry me? Before you say anything, I did in fact plan on asking you to marry me, so it has nothing to do with if you're pregnant or not."

Releasing my hands, he climbs to his feet, walks to his bags, and pulls out a little box from its depths, before returning to me where he once more goes down on one knee and takes hold of my hands in one of his.

Flipping open the box, he repeats his question as I stare in stupefaction at the beautiful amethyst gemstone surrounded by smaller rose zircon stones, nestled in a white gold band, inside the velvet box. I look from the ring to Victor and know this is something he's thought a lot about.

"I chose the amethyst because it reminds me of the color your eyes turn when your magick comes out to play, especially if your wolf is peering out of your eyes," he quickly explains, as if unsure if I like the ring or not. "And the rose zircon because it's your birthstone."

"It's beautiful. I can't believe you found me such a beautiful ring. I love it. Yes, yes, I'll marry you. Oh, Victor, I love you too." I fling my arms around him, and because he was balanced on one knee, I manage to knock us both to the floor, where I take advantage and ravish his mouth.

Soon, though, our hands start exploring each other's bodies once more, and we're making love on the floor. At some stage, Victor puts his ring on my finger and links our hands together as I ride him, my back arching backward as he thrusts from below meeting my body as I impale myself on him.

Our bodies turn slick with sweat, our breaths hitch, and our hearts gallop. I bend forward and kiss him. Breathe in his sent and taste. *God, I love him.*

Chapter 54

Eventually, we shower and dress and wander downstairs to join the others and share our news with them. Well, some of our news anyway. We both agree that we'll only share that we're getting married, not that we believe we might be having a child. That's something we want to keep to ourselves, until we know for sure.

Hand in hand, we practically glide down the staircase. I wouldn't have been surprised to learn that clouds brought us down the stairs, as I'm positive my feet don't touch the ground. Cloud nine has nothing on how I'm feeling right now.

"Hey, how you feeling?" Jezebel asks, upon spotting me descending the stairs. Her gaze is concerned when it lands on me, then sharpens as she must see something that a second later makes relief take its place.

I beam a reassuring grin at her. Releasing Victor's hand, I hurry to my friend and wrap her in my embrace. "I'm really, really good. I saw my spirit guide," I tell her.

"Oh, thank God. Candi, you had us all so worried. I thought we'd lose you, like we did Jasmine there for a while. I couldn't go through that again."

A sob catches in her throat, and I feel tears dampening my neck. I try to lean back to get a proper look at Jezebel, but her arms tighten preventing me from extracting myself.

"Hey, oh Jez, I'm sorry I didn't mean to hurt anyone. I just couldn't deal with…"

Releasing me from her embrace, Jezebel wipes the tears from her cheeks with unsteady hands. Her tear-filled gaze connects with mine as a tremulous smile flits across her lips. "I get it. Honestly, I do. I just couldn't stand the thought of you hurting so much for protecting and saving us all.

"I wish you didn't have to do it, but I'm so grateful you did." Looking over my shoulder, she nods at the vampire behind me. "I'm glad you have one another. And I can't thank you enough, Victor, for being here and loving my friend the way you do. If it weren't for you…"

"What?" Victor's rich voice washes over and through me, curling around my heart and tugs it gently. A moment later, his strong arms wrap around my waist and pull me gently back to rest against him.

"If it weren't for you, I believe we would have lost Candi forever," Jezebel replies.

Her words send ice down my spine. The agony and heartbreak as well as gratitude toward Victor make me realize more than anything else, just how far I'd descended into my world of torment and grief.

"So, thank you, from the bottom of my heart. Thank you for loving her and not giving up on her. But, dude, a word of warning, you have seriously got your hands full with this one." Giving him a slight nod of her head, she turns to walk away, pauses, and without turning around, calls over her shoulder, "If you ever need anything, Victor, I'll help you. All you need to do is ask." With that, she struts into the lounge.

We stand there back to front for a while, letting Jezebel's words sink into us, before finally with a gentle squeeze of his fingers around my waist, Victor releases me. Linking our hands, he leads me through the door Jezebel just entered.

Silence greets us as our friends turn toward us. Slowly, as if they're uncertain if they should, they advance toward us.

"I'm okay. Honestly," I reassure them, to which I receive relieved sighs and mutters of "Thank God for that."

"You had us so worried," Jasmine chides me, before advancing toward me and hugging me. Wrapping my arms around her, I give her a reassuring hug back. A moment later, the other girls have launched themselves at us and join in. Slowly, we disentangle ourselves from one another.

"Don't ever do that again. I honestly don't think my poor heart, or Victor's, could handle you going AWOL again," exclaims Nancy, giving me a slight shake of the shoulders before once more wrapping me in her embrace.

"Ditto to that," mutters T.T. with a tremulous smile flitting across her lips. A moment later, she lets out a slight gasp and grabs my left hand. "Holy hell in a bucket of ice, does this mean what I think it does?" Her gaze locking with mine in joyous surprise.

"Yes, it does," Victor replies, with a smirk of such satisfaction on his face, I can't help the bubble of laughter from gurgling up and bursting out of me. "Candi has done me the honor of agreeing to become my bride."

Squeals of delight reach deafening volumes as congratulations are issued all around. With an arm wrapped around my gorgeous vampire consort, I show everyone my ring, and a feeling of pure bliss envelops me.

This moment is what we were all fighting for, to love and celebrate our love for our partners no matter who or what they are. This is what so many died for, and as long as The Protectors remain, will continue to fight and die for. This simple right to love unconditionally and be loved in return.

A simple right, an honest one, and to be honest, a beautiful one too. Looking at Victor and our friends, I know deep in my heart the war isn't over and that I will do anything to protect those I love and those I will never meet so everyone can have this moment and a love like ours.

As if he senses my thoughts and emotions, I feel Victor's arm tighten around my waist, and when I glance toward him, he inclines his head ever so slightly. "We're in this together, forever. No matter what, beautiful. One day, we will win the war; the Prophecy will come true." Victor's voice reverberates in my head. His words a caress and promise.

Through our bond, I reply, "I know we are. I'm not afraid anymore, of us. Our bond, our love for each other. I can't wait to explore our lives together, and I hope more than I could ever imagine that we will have a child. Timing sucks though. I just gotta say that," I add, to which the man I love more than I ever dreamt possible bursts out laughing.

"Hey, what's funny?" demands Felicity. "If you're doing that bond thing," she adds while waving her fingers between us for extra emphasize, "then that's so not fair! Seriously, though, what's going on?"

"We're just excited and happy," I reply, feeling a slight tinge of guilt at not sharing the fact that we believe/hope I'm pregnant. But the thought that we might be wrong—after all, the chances are...well, almost impossible. That depressing thought feels like a bucket of icy water being thrown over me. Almost as if seeing a miracle and finding out later you didn't see what you thought you did.

Before my thoughts can descend farther down the self-pity of delusion-ville path they're on, Vlad strides into the room. Upon seeing me, his nostrils flare and his eyes widen, before flickering down to my stomach.

"*Dumnezeule, tu eşti insarcinata!* My God, you're pregnant!" In an exclamation of shocked wonder, Vlad's words explode from his mouth, creating deafening silence into the stunned room.

Chapter 55

The silence lasts for a grand total of two seconds before chaos reigns in the room.

"You're what?"

"How? I mean, I know how...but how?"

"Oh my God, really? Wow, just wow!"

My friends' questions tumble over one another, and to be honest, I can't figure out who is asking what, as their voices blend into each other's, and all I can think is, *I'm pregnant*. A wave of protectiveness washes over me for my unborn child, and instinctively, I glance toward Victor and see the joy and wonderment wash over his features, mirroring mine.

"Enough." Dragging me slightly behind him, Victor manages to quieten the room with one word, delivered in a tone a drill sergeant would envy.

Peeking around Victor's broad shoulders, I let my gaze rove over my friends until it lands on the vampire who'd caused the ruckus in the first place.

"Vlad, nice to see you too. Fancy expanding a bit on your comment?" My voice sounds like a languid drawl, calm and cool, as if I was offering him tea instead of asking he explain what the hell he said, and how he could possibly know I'm pregnant for sure, when even I didn't know!

"My apologies, *doamna mea*, my lady," murmurs Vlad, placing a fisted right hand over his chest he bows at me. "I didn't mean to cause a commotion. I can sense your child inside you. Your child's power beats like a living heartbeat, strong and powerful, like nothing I've ever felt before."

"You can sense our child?" demands Victor. Shock reverberates in his voice, his arm that had held me protectively behind me, now pulls me to his side and curls around my waist, as his other hand, trembling slightly touches my stomach.

"*Da*, yes, I can sense your baby. *Felicitări*, congratulations."

When I look Vlad in the eyes, I'm surprised to see a shimmer of tears, until I remember he was a father.

"Vlad—" I begin to offer condolences toward his loss. As if he knows what I'm thinking, he interrupts me before I can say any more.

"*Nu*, no, you mistake my tears. It's not sadness but joy they're for. Everything we've been fighting for, all the losses we've suffered, I now finally see an end in sight. The Prophecy is coming to fruition. Slowly, *da*, yes, but it's coming."

"Omigod," splutters T.T. Her eyes stretch wide at the corners as everything Vlad says seems to sink into her head, as it is in mine too. "Omigod," she repeats. Turning toward Vlad, she grasps hold of his arm and slightly shakes it before demanding in a whispery voice, "You're right, aren't you?"

"Of course I am!" Vlad growls while glaring at my friend's hand that is currently grabbing his arm. Realizing she isn't paying any attention, he takes hold of her hand as if to pry it from him. Except the moment his bare hand touches hers, something happens. Both suck in a breath, and their eyes connect with each other's. I stare in surprise at the scene enfolding before my eyes. Honestly, it's like watching a romantic film come to life before my very eyes. Totally unexpected and rather beautiful all at the same time.

"*Nu m-am gândit*…I never thought…" Trailing off what he was about to say, Vlad traces the contours of T.T.'s face with the back of his fingers and rubs his thumb over her lips with the hand not clamping hers to his arm.

"You never thought what?" T.T. inquires as she stares with a look of awe and confusion on her face at the prince before her.

"*Că voi găsi pe cineva să iubească din nou.*"

"Huh?" my eloquent friend blurts out, making me want to snicker.

"That I would find someone to love again," Vlad repeats, this time in English.

"Oh." The words leave T.T.'s mouth sounding more like a sigh with sounds than words themselves. A light blush rises to her cheeks, and she takes a tiny step closer to Vlad.

Their moment of newfound discovery is interrupted by Jezebel. Her quiet words blast through the room as if she'd shouted them instead of whispered them. "Why now?"

Everyone turns to look at her with expressions of surprise and puzzlement.

"Why now, what?" inquires Cedrix from beside her. His words are soothing, controlled, yet puzzlement and a bit of steel too laces his tone.

Glancing up at him, she bestows on him a smile of such joy and pleasure it makes him blink, and the tension in his jaw which I hadn't noticed before eases.

"Finding love, new life, all this…" She trails off as if searching for the right word before continuing, "…for lack of a better word, joy. It's almost as if our whole lives, we've all been in a limbo of sorts, fighting for survival, and now suddenly the pause button has been taken off, and everything pure and wonderful is happening. Why now though, you know?"

"Because things can be held off for only so long before the world forces life to move on. This has been a hell of a long pause, centuries long, and with everything that has happened—Candi being born and reaching adulthood, the war with *The Protectors*, soul mates finding one another—it's time," Janna informs us all in such a matter-of-fact tone no one can deny her words.

"Like the wheel of life, you can only be in one position for so long before you're forced to move to the next one," Felicity murmurs, her agreement causing us all to look at her. "What? Oh, come off it, that tarot card is so accurate it's frightening at times," she exclaims before carrying on, "and none of you can disagree with that either."

"Wouldn't dream of it," Vivian drawls, raising her hands as if to ward off any further comments. Yet it's the flicker of hope and the softening of her features that cause no more comments to be made. Instead, we all gravitate toward each other, with smiles and grins trembling on our lips and hope for better times in our steps.

Chapter 56

Eight Months Later

"Victor, stop hovering, I'm fine. Honestly," I declare rubbing my extended belly in gentle circles to ease our baby's excited movements. The words have just left my mouth when another spasm makes me groan, this time almost doubling me over with the pain. "Holy shit," I exclaim, as water gushes from between my legs.

"Sweetheart, you're not okay. Our baby is coming!" exclaims Victor. Next thing I know, I'm scooped up by my husband and flitted to the hospital.

"I'm not ready, though," I wail as I burst into tears, burying my face into the side of his neck as my arms tighten around his shoulders.

"Shhhh, it's okay. Everything will be okay," he soothes me, while kicking open the door to the hospital and rushing me over to the nearest doctor he can find. "My wife's water broke, and she's been having some pain," he growls at the exhausted-looking man.

"She'll need to go the maternity ward…"

"But I'm not due for another month. I'm not ready yet," is the only thing I manage to say, as if my declaring that simple fact can convince my baby to stay inside me.

When another wave of pain slices through me, I

have the sudden realization that the fact I'm not ready means diddly-squat. Apparently, our child is more than ready to come into the world.

****

For eight months, I've been following my cousin from a distance. Paradise Falls has turned into a Protectors-*free zone. Somehow, Candi and her friends know when any member is around and have hunted them down. After a couple of months of this, word got through from the top circle to stay away from the town until further notice.*

Receiving a phone call from a contact of mine that my cousin was rushed into the hospital, I take a chance and slip into the town. Somehow, she's pregnant. Logic whispers in my head she must have slept with someone other than the vampire, yet I know deep down inside where my fear resides, that isn't the case. This child is what all the fear has been about for centuries. This child will bring the end to me and all my kind. All who are part of The Protectors.

****

"Only take the oxygen during contractions," the midwife informs me, as she tries to remove the happy gas from me.

"I'm having it all the time!" I growl back at her, refusing to relinquish my hold on the mask.

"You're okay, sweetheart. Just breathe." Victor tries to sooth me, as he squeezes the hand he's holding gently.

"Don't you talk to me; it's your fault I'm— owwww, shit that hurt!" I exclaim, tightening my hand around his. I feel my fingers stiffen from their curled-up position, where they wrap around his hand.

236

"I love you, you complete arse," I blubber a moment later before inhaling the gas once more.

"I love you too." His amused voice rumbles through me, reaching me from my perch on the pink fluffy cloud I'm currently floating on.

"Okay, you'll have to take that from her now. We're ready for her to push," declares a voice from between my legs. A moment later, the crafty nurse beside me snatches the mask from me and hides it behind her.

"Okay, Candi, I need you to push. Remember your breathing, it'll help," the nurse informs me.

Throwing her a baleful glance, I sit up a little more, panting as I was previously instructed. I start bearing down at the same time.

Victor wraps an arm around my back to help support me and does the Lamaze breathing with me.

Gratitude and love sweep through me, followed by exhaustion. I'm not sure how long I've been in labor. Reaching a hand out, I trace the contours of my gorgeous vampire husband and whisper my love for him. Stunning silvery-green eyes meet mine, as a wail from our newborn child erupts into the room.

"Congratulations, you have a daughter," informs the midwife a second later as she brings our swaddled baby girl to me. Feeling dizzy, I manage to graze my fingers against her tiny ones before darkness envelops me.

****

Hours I've been pacing the corridors of this blasted hospital, when finally, I hear the wail of a newborn baby, followed a second later by a roar of anguish and an alarm going off. My heart freezes in shock as I realize that everything my cousin has gone through has been brought down by her child.

Surely, I must be mistaken. No way can someone so vibrant and filled with so much power be killed, not in battle, but in childbirth. A moment later, the earth vibrates, the walls tremble, and a blast of pure white light erupts around the doorframe leading to the delivery room right before it's blasted off its hinges.

A wind howls through the corridors bringing destruction and fear in its wake. "What the hell?" *is the only thing I manage to exclaim before I'm blasted against a wall column. As the light touches me, I feel it sink into my skin and hear screams of terror from all those connected to me through the blood-link I share with those on the third level of* The Protectors. *A scream of pain erupts from me…*

****

Oh my God, I'm drinking my nurse as if she's a juice box. Retracting my fangs, I let her drop to the floor, only a second later to realize I have fangs!

"What the fuck just happened?" I ask the stunned-looking vampire beside me.

"You died." His hoarse voice barely manages to say the words aloud, and I'm surprised to see blood tracks on his cheeks from where he'd cried. Then Victor's words penetrate my brain.

"Say what?" Shaking my head as if to dislodge something covering my ears, I repeat my question.

"Sweetheart, you died. I thought I'd lost you forever." A shudder ripples through him as he chokes on the words, and that's the moment I realize, I really had died.

"So how am I here, and why was I drinking my

nurse as if she was a can of soda?" I demand, feeling slightly terrified. Okay, totally petrified to be completely honest.

"I don't know..." He turns to look in the corner to where the terrified-looking midwife is currently making shushing noises to the gurgling baby in her arms. "Your fingers brushed our daughter's, and then you just..."

"Died," I finish for him.

Turning back to me, he gathers me in his arms and murmurs, "But only for a moment. Everything went crazy. I thought at first we were having an earthquake until you burned brightly with a blinding white light. And I realized you were somehow causing it.

"Your power blasted from you, surrounded you, and then you were sinking fangs into the nurse there."

Leaning over the bed, I look down at the unconscious woman. Reaching out to her, I filter healing light into her as I whisper an apology for...well, eating her. A second later, she sits up and looks bemusedly around as if trying to figure out why she's on the floor.

"Oh, oh my God!" she exclaims in a tone of voice filled with wonderment.

Feeling puzzled, I glance toward the midwife and then Victor. Seeing both their bemused expressions, I know I won't find any answers there.

"Are you okay?" I tentively ask her.

"I feel it—oh my God, I can feel my magick." Turning to look at me, she stares at me with a mixture of wonderment and awe. "You gave me my magic, or let it loose somehow. Thank you."

"Denise, you were born a dud. You don't have any..." The midwife's words trail off as Denise conjures a glass of water and drinks it.

"Ahhh." Smacking her lips, she gives the shocked midwife a baleful glare. "I'm no dud anymore, so don't ever call me one again." Picking herself up off the floor, she glances toward me, thanks me, and then leaves.

I notice the speculative look the woman in the corner throws me and then my daughter. Victor must have noticed it too, for he quickly leaves my side and takes our daughter from her.

Climbing gingerly from the bed, I reach Victor's side a moment later and look properly for the first time into my daughter's face. Silvery-violet eyes meet mine, and a rosebud mouth opens to let out a tired yawn. I feel tears well up as I stare in awe at the most beautiful baby I have ever seen.

Looking up into the proud father holding her, I feel my heart burst open and overflow with the amount of love I feel for my child and husband. Together, we leave the room and enter the destroyed hallway.

In shock, we stare about the place. I notice the body of a man crumpled against a pillar. Going by the destruction of the place, I wouldn't have thought too much about it, except for the spider-web lines covering every inch of visible skin.

Somehow, I instinctively know that he was a member of *The Protectors,* and I'm guessing that when I died and came back, the Prophecy came true.

"I do believe we should get your clothes and leave," Victor mutters to me, while staring at the body. A moment later, he's checked us out. We both know the only reason we were allowed to leave is because the hospital staff are still trying to sort out the damage created by my magick.

We've just gotten back home, thanks to Victor flitting us here, when I hear my phone ringing. Answering it, I listen to what's been said which causes me to almost drop it a moment later. Turning to Victor, I repeat what Selena had just told me. "Nancy's eyes have changed color. They're now blue again with a brown ring circling them. She's both a zombie and a necromancer."

Epilogue

October 31, 2014

Dear Journal,
So much has happened in the last twenty-four hours. Victor and I are the proud parents of a beautiful baby girl. We've called her Cynthia-Marie, after both our mothers. She's so tiny and delicate, yet the power inside her is immense. She is the Triple Magick one from the Prophecy, and I am the second one.

I never understood what it had meant when it said, "When the Double Magick one fails to rise again, then there will be two Triple Magick ones." It was only when I died after giving birth to Cynthia-Marie and came back to life, fangs in the neck of my nurse—not my finest hour—that I finally got it. For my third type of magick to come to me, I had to die.

Anyway, I'm now a badass witch, wolf, and vampire. Hell, yeah, I'm totally awesome, and so is my precious bundle of joy.

The magick is returning to those who lost it due to being turned into a vampire or zombie, or awakening in those classified as duds. I never realized that Victor was a werewolf before he was turned into a vampire. One day Victor, Cynthia-Marie, and I will be able to run together as a pack, how awesome is that.

Talking of which, I had a phone call from

Transylvania. Guess who's the big wolf once more; yeah, that's right. Vlad's the alpha wolf once more, as well as being a badass vampire, and newly engaged to T.T.

And they're not the only ones.

Kheda then popped the question, and Jasmine accepted. They've both moved into Jasmine's old family home. The renovations were completed last week.

Selena and Dante are also moving in together, and I know he's going to ask her to marry him soon. I helped pick out the ring, and it's beautiful.

Jezebel has become a bounty hunter and is working with her husband Cedrix. They got married a couple of weeks ago. Between cases believe it or not.

Nancy, Vivian, and Felicity are off traveling together. I think they mentioned something about bodies in the Amazon and a missing prince. Not too sure, to be honest, if I heard that right, though. They did promise to be back for Christmas. I can't wait for everyone to meet Cynthia-Marie.

I just caught the news before coming upstairs to write in you. There've been a lot of unexplained deaths. People just dropping dead. They go suddenly but not quietly, all found screaming and bearing a spider-web mark.

I'm guessing, they were all on the same blood-link level as the dead man in the hospital. I can't get him out of my head. I feel as if I've seen him somewhere before, but I just can't put my finger on where.

Anyway, this will be the last time I write in you for a while. I'll be busy changing nappies and being a mum. The war against The Protectors *isn't over, but for now, Victor and I are taking a time out from it, unless it comes to us. Our priority is our beautiful daughter, making sure she's safe and has us here with her.*

Until the next time I write in you.

Candi Harlow

P.S. Happy thirty-first birthday to me.

A word from the author...

Born in Dublin, I moved to England, then finally back home to Ireland. I now live in West Cork but want to move to America.

In October 2010, I self-published a book of poetry called *Different Kinds of Emotions*.

But I always wanted to write down the stories in my head, until finally I did. My first novel is a paranormal fantasy called *Double Magick in the Falls*, Book One in the Candi Reynolds Series.

When I was a child, I fell in love with books, amazing stories filled with mystery and intrigue, danger and fantasy. This love has progressed into a passion with me. I also like photography and cemeteries—the older the better.

aprilhollingworth.wix.com/april-hollingworth